T0197173

THIRD IDENTITY

Kelsey Gjesdal

WestBow
P R E S S®
A DIVISION OF THOMAS NELSON
& ZONDERVAN

WestBow Press books may be ordered through booksellers or by contacting:

WestBow Press
A Division of Thomas Nelson & Zondervan
1663 Liberty Drive
Bloomington, IN 47403
www.westbowpress.com
844-714-3454

Scripture quotations taken from the New American Standard Bible® (NASB), Copyright © 1960, 1962, 1963, 1968, 1971, 1972, 1973, 1975, 1977, 1995 by The Lockman Foundation Used by permission. www.Lockman.org

ISBN: 978-1-9736-6506-9 (sc)
ISBN: 978-1-9736-6505-2 (hc)
ISBN: 978-1-9736-6507-6 (e)

Library of Congress Control Number: 2019906979

Print information available on the last page.

WestBow Press rev. date: 04/16/2024

CHAPTER 1

Ring! Ring!

I forced my eyes open and sat up, glancing at the clock. 3:27 a.m.

"Are you kidding me?" I grumbled, crawling out of bed. I made my way over to my desk as the ringing continued. I plopped down into the chair, grabbed my headphones, and clicked the answer button on my computer. "What's up?" I spoke into the mic on my headphones. "If this isn't urgent, I'm hanging up and going to bed."

"You will not hang up under any circumstances!" Mr. Brian said.

I sighed. "What is it this time?" My boss had a habit of creating issues with the electronics in his office building. I, being his technology assistant, was constantly being called in at random hours of the day or night to fix things.

"This is extremely important!" he replied, sounding urgent.

"I'm listening," I said, bracing myself for bad news.

"I was reviewing the quarterly systems check that you and Jason ran, and we have a problem. It looks like someone is leaking information to other companies."

Now I was fully awake. "Really? Who is it?"

"I don't know. That's why I need you. You need to figure this out, or our company will suffer some serious blows."

"I can do that," I said coolly. "I'll be there early tomorrow. See ya."

"All right. Goodnight, Amelia."

I clicked the call off.

I leaned back in my chair and sighed. I hadn't done a good job covering my tracks. Sure, Mr. Brian had no idea my name wasn't Amelia and that I was also working for his biggest rival, Mr. Zaiden. But now he knew someone was giving away information to rival companies. What he couldn't find out was who that somebody was—me.

Forcing myself to stay awake, I called Mr. Zaiden. He answered promptly. "Hello? Richard Zaiden."

"It's me—Mariah," I replied. Mr. Zaiden didn't really know my identity either; it was better and safer that way. I thought for a moment before continuing. "So we've got a problem with Brian."

"Let me guess. You didn't cover up your work very well before the quarterly systems check, right?"

I rolled my eyes. "How'd you know?"

Mr. Zaiden chuckled. "I sent you on that mission, remember? You didn't have time to do both, did you?"

"Not really, so technically this is your fault," I replied. *I'm surprised he didn't think of this before he sent me on that dumb mission*, I thought.

"Actually, it's Lisa's fault. I asked her to hack into Brian's system and make sure everything looked smooth, but she didn't do a thorough job," Mr. Zaiden informed me.

I smiled, relieved. "So the evidence will lead to Lisa, and I'm off the hook?"

"No, the evidence will need to be redirected. Otherwise

both you and Lisa are in trouble. And I can't lose my best agent, can I?"

"Well, who's your best agent?" I asked with a smirk, already knowing the answer.

"Hmm." He paused, sounding thoughtful. "Well, I always thought Lisa was top quality."

"Yeah, right. She's the laziest agent I have ever worked with."

"Of course you're my best agent," Mr. Zaiden said, laughing. "And you're right about Lisa. She needs to work on her initiative and drive. Now why don't you show off your own skills and fix this problem. I'm assuming you'll need to work at Brian's tomorrow—I mean, today—to get this worked out."

"Yup."

"Then you can have the day off here. Now get some rest so you can do a quality job tomorrow. I have confidence in you."

"All right, thanks. Bye," I said, turning the call off. I took off the headphones and walked back over to my bed. *And I thought I'd have a low-key day tomorrow*, I thought as I tumbled into bed.

🔫

My alarm went off way too early that morning. I wanted to hit the snooze button and skip going to work, but I knew that would be a dumb move. I got out of bed and ate breakfast; then I got ready for work. I pulled out my clothes for the day, a classy business-lady outfit. After putting it on and pinning my "Amelia" name tag onto it, I began pinning my long, wavy brown hair on top of my head. After it was all secured, I pulled out a shoulder-length, blonde wig and secured it in place. I checked to make sure the wig looked as natural as possible, then pulled out my makeup. I got out my temporary blonde dye and dyed my eyebrows blonde to match the wig. I quickly applied my makeup, grabbed my work purse, put my shoes on, and headed out the door.

The walk to Mr. Brian's office buildings took only fifteen minutes. As I walked, I looked at the streets next to me and the sky above. There was early-morning traffic like usual. The impatient drivers crowded the streets with their cars, while the richer, impatient pilots flew their personal aircrafts to work. They made me laugh. Sometimes I got to work faster by walking than the people did by driving.

I walked up to the front doors of Mr. Brian's office building and found them already unlocked, so I hurried in. I went straight to Mr. Brian's office. Before I even knocked on the door, he opened it and said, "Come in! I'm glad you got here early."

Mr. Brian was average height, a little on the heavier side, with graying hair. He was always serious and professional, but today his green eyes looked worried. "We're in big trouble," he said as he sat down behind his desk. I closed the door and went to sit across from him.

"Look here," he said, pulling a file out from a drawer. "This is the list of business interactions other companies have done with Patrick Brian's Power Company."

"It's looking good," I replied, scanning the sheet. "This must be the corrected copy that you show potential customers?"

"Yes, ma'am," Mr. Brain said. "We do have an uncorrected file of the PBPC interactions—"

"—in the safe," I finished. "I know because you asked me to enter last year's files into the computer a while back."

"I remember," Brian replied impatiently. "I was going to have you enter this year's files into the computer after we ran the security check, just to make sure last year's interactions were still safe."

"So what's the problem?" I asked. But I already knew the answer.

Brian sighed. "One of our employees gave an outsider access to those files. I've been doing everything I can to figure out who did it, but I can't. That's why I need you. You need to find out who did this. This security breach could mean the end of Patrick Brian's Power Company if the wrong person gets their hands on those files."

I nodded, understanding Mr. Brian's concern. PBPC was a well-known company, and it raked in a good amount of cash. Actually, it was more than a good amount because Mr. Brian knew how to fudge the numbers and still look professional. If any of his customers knew he stole money from them, the company would be shut down. Those who knew about the scam, including me, were on those records. But as long as the information wasn't given out to any customers and I did a good job with the cover-up, Mr. Brian would think everything was fine, and I'd walk away clean.

"I've tracked down people who've done this kind of thing before," I told him with a smile. "This will be a piece of cake."

Brian nodded solemnly. "Good. Get to work then, and I'll be back to check on you in an hour. The computer's already logged in." He stood and reached out his hand.

"Thanks," I replied as I shook his hand.

I watched him leave the room, hearing him say under his breath, "How an eighteen-year-old girl has experience in tracking people on computers, I'll never know. Kids seem to know it all these days."

I smirked as I sat down in Mr. Brian's chair. *I'm not your average girl. Your average eighteen-year-old is still in college. You don't see me sitting in school, now do ya?* I thought. *All right, now it's time to focus. This is more than just finding the whodunit. It's time to pick whodunit.*

I scrolled through a list of names of people who worked for PBPC, and the name Jason Lenard caught my eye. *Ah, the new guy,* I thought. *What an easy target.*

🔫

"How is it going, Amelia?" Mr. Brian said as he entered the room.

I turned to face him and smiled. "It's going well. I seem to have a few leads. I'll keep following them and let you know what I come up with. It does appear to be an inside job."

He nodded thoughtfully. "I thought it would be. The security is too tight to be otherwise. Now, do you have your suspicions on who's behind this?"

I shrugged. "Yeah, I have my suspicions, but I'll wait to see if they're confirmed."

"All right then. I'll leave you to your work. Let me know when you've got it figured out," Mr. Brian said as he exited the room.

I turned back to my work. So far it was easy to replace my work with Jason's username. In just a few hours, I would tell Mr. Brian who had hacked the computers.

🔫

Later that afternoon I called Mr. Brian to let him know I'd found the culprit. I smiled to myself. *That was pretty good,* I thought. *Probably the fastest cover-up job you've done so far.*

Mr. Brian entered his office. "All right, who's our culprit?"

"Take a look for yourself." I pointed at the computer screen.

Mr. Brian looked over the computer screen and then looked at me. "You're saying that Jason Lenard is our man?" He sighed. "He's a hard worker. Are you sure he did this?"

"Positive," I replied. "But another thing you need to know is that he gave some of this information to a few of your customers. What are you going to do about that?"

"Hmm ... I suppose we'll tell them that one of our employees was undercover for a rival company and gave out false information," Mr. Brian suggested.

"That would work," I agreed.

"But we need evidence. We need to see Jason in the act of changing the files," Mr. Brian said.

"Are you serious?" I asked, starting to feel nervous. I pointed at the computer screen. "Isn't this enough evidence?"

"No," Mr. Brian replied seriously. "I want our customers to be assured that they aren't getting ripped off. We need video surveillance of Jason changing the records. I want you to help me get this."

"Yes, sir," I replied, acting confident, but inside I had no idea how to get that video.

As I walked home from work, I phoned Mr. Zaiden. "Hey boss, it's Mariah."

"Oh, hello. Did you get your tracks covered?" he asked.

"Yes, that much I did, but I have a problem now," I replied. "I framed a new guy so that this random security breach would make sense. It was perfect, except now Brian wants video surveillance of Jason stealing the files and sending them to customers."

"That's unexpected," Mr. Zaiden replied. "But don't worry. I've got experience in this sort of thing. If you have time to stop by my office tonight, I can help you form a plan."

"I can be there in twenty minutes," I said.

"See you then," Mr. Zaiden replied, then hung up. I quickened my pace. Mr. Zaiden's office was on the other side of town. I didn't like going there in the evenings since I was alone, and it was in the bad part of town; however, this was urgent.

In less than twenty minutes, I arrived. The building was inside a fenced-in area. I pulled my security card out of my purse and scanned it at the front gate. The gate swung open, and I headed for the large concrete building in the center of the property. At the front door, I scanned my card again, and the door unlocked. Zaiden's office was on the fifth floor. Since there was no elevator, I hurried up the stairs.

Mr. Zaiden met me at the top of the stairs. He was a friendly, middle-aged man with very dark hair and eyes. He was of average height but extremely muscular—you knew he wasn't one to mess around with.

"Two minutes late," he said with a grin. "And still in disguise. Your attention to detail amazes me."

I'd forgotten that I was still disguised as Amelia, but that didn't matter. Mr. Zaiden had seen me disguised as Amelia plenty of times.

I was breathing hard after almost running the stairs. "You should get an elevator," I said. "Then I wouldn't be late."

He laughed. "If I had an elevator, then this building wouldn't be as secure." I nodded in agreement. "Now come with me. I've already thought of a plan to get that video footage you need."

🔫

"Okay, message sent," I said, putting my phone back into my purse.

"Good. If he agrees, then the plan is in motion," Mr. Zaiden replied.

"Thanks for your help." I stood to leave when my phone beeped. I pulled it back out of my purse. "That was Jason. It looks like the plan is on."

I headed out of the building, accompanied by a security guard. Since it was late and I needed to get to the PBPC building before Jason, Mr. Zaiden had one of his security guards drive me. I got there just as Mr. Brian was leaving the building. *Right on time*, I thought, knowing how punctual Mr. Brian was.

The security guard dropped me off behind the building in an area where I knew there was a blind spot for the security cameras. Normally the security system was flawless, but recently a road construction crew had knocked down a camera at the back corner of the property. I was scheduled to fix it this week, but due to Mr. Brian's discovery of the security leak, I didn't have time to fix both problems. *Lucky me*, I thought gratefully.

I ran up to the building and pulled open the nearest first-floor window, which led into the girls' bathroom. I quietly opened the bathroom door and slipped into the hall leading to the stairs. Staying in the shadows, I climbed the stairs to the third floor and went straight to the security office. Once there, I switched the security cameras in the computer room to a picture of the room and set a timer for five minutes. Then

I hurried to the computer room and after a little hacking pulled up the unedited files of Mr. Brian's scams. I checked my watch. 9:42.

Jason should be here in three minutes, I told myself.

After returning to the security room and making sure the picture was switched back to the live footage, I sat down and waited. At 9:47 Jason's car pulled into the parking lot on the camera monitor. He got out of his car while talking on his phone and hung up when he reached the door. He pulled on the door handle, and that's when I realized—the door. I hadn't unlocked the door! I switched all the security cameras to picture mode except those outside the building and then raced for the door.

Good thing I told him I'd be here, I thought.

I got to the door and unlocked it. "Sorry about that," I said as he entered.

"No problem," Jason replied, smiling. I'd never actually spoken to him before, but I'd seen him around. Something about Jason seemed so familiar, but I couldn't place it. He had brown eyes and hair, and was fairly tall and skinny, not terribly muscular. He almost looked like a teenager, possibly my own age, but I assumed he must be older than he looked.

"I'm glad you came," I said as we walked back down the hall toward the elevator. "One of the computers is down, and I need some help unhooking it so we can get it replaced with a new one. You were the only person willing to help. I appreciate this."

I knew my face and voice showed appreciation, but I felt nothing of the sort. Instead I felt anxiety and a twinge of guilt, but I knew this was the job of a double agent. *Sometimes a double agent needs to do dirty work, even if it's not her first choice*, I told myself.

"Do you always work late nights?" Jason asked as the elevator went up. "I mean, past nine o'clock is unusual."

I shrugged. "Not usually, but I had some work that I needed to get finished up today."

"Deadlines," Jason said, shaking his head. "A love-hate relationship."

"Sure," I replied, not sure what he meant. We stepped off the elevator onto the third floor and headed to the computer room. "You go on ahead. I need to grab some tools I left in the security room."

He nodded and headed down the hall. I entered the security room and turned all the cameras back to normal mode, watching Jason through the screen. He walked into the computer room and flicked on the lights. *Not exactly sneaky looking,* I thought, *but then again most of the hackers I know are pretty cocky. I think this will work.*

Jason looked around the room; I assumed he was trying to figure out which computer was being replaced when he noticed the computer that was turned on. He walked over to it and started reading. His eyes widened, and I read his lips. "Whoa!" He kept mumbling to himself, but I couldn't tell what he said. Then he glanced around, put a finger to his ear, and began talking. He nodded a few times, then started typing on the keyboard.

I zoomed in on the computer to see what he was doing. *He's sending the information to someone,* I thought excitedly. *This is perfect evidence!* After he'd sent his work, he appeared to continue talking. Then he called me. "Are you bringing those tools?"

I didn't answer; instead I hid behind one of the desks. Jason walked into the room, calling, "Amelia! Hey, where'd you go?"

I held my breath and finally heard him leave, still calling for me.

I cautiously slipped out of my hiding place and watched him get back into the elevator. Then I turned off the video footage again, hurrying over to the stairs. I met Jason on the second floor near my office.

"I thought you were getting your tools from the security room," Jason said. He still smiled, but he eyed me suspiciously.

"Turns out they were in my office," I replied. I picked up the small toolbox lying on the floor; it was actually my coworker's tools, but Jason couldn't possibly know that. "Let's get to work."

"You're sure you don't need a ride home?" Jason asked as we left the building. "It's really late."

"I'm fine," I answered, "but thanks for the offer. I don't live far from here, and I enjoy the walk."

Jason looked at me quizzically but replied, "All right. I guess I'll see you later."

"Bye!" I said with a wave. I watched Jason leave the parking lot, then called Mr. Brian. "Hey, Mr. Brian, this is Amelia. I have some important information for you. I need you to meet me in the security room at the PBPC office. When can you be there?" After he told me he'd be there in fifteen minutes, I hung up and raced back into the security room to get the video ready.

A short time later, Mr. Brian rushed into the security room. "This had better be urgent. You realize, Amelia, that it's eleven o'clock and that normal people would be at home—"

"You'll be glad I called you," I interrupted, "because I have important information for you. I found our culprit."

"Were you here spying tonight?" Mr. Brian asked. I couldn't tell by his face whether he was impressed or disturbed.

"Well, yeah, spying from home," I lied, "but that doesn't matter. This video is what you need to see."

I showed him the video of Jason looking at the files and e-mailing them to someone. Afterward Mr. Brian shook his head and said, "Bravo, Amelia. This is just the evidence we need."

I sighed with relief. "I'm glad we figured this out," I said, but inwardly I was rejoicing over not getting caught.

"I need you to be in my office tomorrow morning at ten," Mr. Brian said as we headed downstairs. "I want you to be there when I speak with Jason."

"Yes, sir," I replied, grinning.

The next morning at ten o'clock sharp, I entered Mr. Brian's office. "Good morning!" I said cheerfully.

"Good morning to you," Mr. Brian replied sarcastically, then spoke into his intercom. "Jason Lenard to my office, please."

Jason showed up a few minutes later. "Yes, sir?" he said as he entered the room.

"Take a seat," Mr. Brian said, motioning to the chair next to mine.

Jason glanced worriedly at me. "Oh no. Did we hook up the computer wrong?"

I shook my head as Mr. Brian began to speak.

"Mr. Lenard, we have a video of you tampering with some of PBPC's records last night at 9:56 p.m.," Mr. Brian said.

"Tampering with records? What are you talking about?" Jason asked, confused.

"You sent out some of our records by e-mail without permission—records that had been changed to say that PBPC has been stealing money from its customers," Mr. Brian continued.

Jason opened his mouth to speak, but Mr. Brian raised a hand to stop him. "Let me show you this video, and then we'll hear what you have to say." He turned his computer toward us so we could watch. When it was over, Mr. Brian asked, "Is that you in this video?"

"It is," Jason replied slowly as he fidgeted with his watch.

"So you admit to changing the records and sending them out?" Mr. Brian asked. I had a sinking feeling in my stomach. *Jason didn't change any records*, I thought. *He only sent out the real ones ... and so did I.*

"Sir, I didn't change any records," Jason stated calmly. "I was helping Amelia install a computer, and while she went to get her tools, I saw those records up on the computer."

"Wait, Amelia, you were here installing a new computer?" Mr. Brian cut in. "There are no videos of you in the building until after he left."

"He's lying," I replied. Jason's jaw dropped as he stared at me. He knew I was the one really lying. "I told you I was monitoring the security system from home."

"Jason, if you tell the truth, this will make things easier for us," Mr. Brian said sternly.

"I was here installing a computer with Amelia. I saw the records on the computer and sent them to ... uh, a friend of mine. I did not change the records. I'm telling the truth," Jason said, looking Mr. Brian in the eye.

Mr. Brian sighed. He sat, staring at his hands. After what seemed like an eternity, he said, "I was hoping I wouldn't have to say this, but Jason, you're fired." He pressed a button on his intercom and said, "Security, please escort Mr. Lenard out of the building." Instantly one of the security guards entered, grabbed Jason's arm, and pulled him out of the room.

"Good job, Amelia," Mr. Brian said, a hint of a smile on his face. "Now everything can go back to normal. I knew I could count on you."

I smiled as brightly as I could. "Thank you, sir."

"I guess this deserves a bonus," Mr. Brian said, unlocking the safe under his desk. He pulled out a stack of hundred-dollar bills and pushed it across his desk toward me.

I picked up the stack and flipped through the bills. "Wow."

"Don't spend it all at once," Mr. Brian replied. "Now, after you fix the broken camera in the back of the property, your work is done for today."

🔫

Fixing the camera took hardly any time, and pretty soon I was back at home. I pulled my wig off and plopped down on the couch. Part of me was excited. I'd gotten away clean with a bonus.

But the other part of me felt horrible. Jason hadn't gotten away clean. *But it doesn't matter,* I told myself, pushing my guilt aside. *When you have a job like this, you have to take risks and pay the price. That's how it works.*

CHAPTER 2

Later that afternoon, I got a call from Mr. Zaiden. "Hello, this is Mariah speaking," I said as I set down the newspaper I'd been reading.

"Did the plan work?" Mr. Zaiden said quickly.

"Yeah, it was fine," I replied.

"So everything's good with Brian? He's not suspicious of you?" Mr. Zaiden asked. His voice sounded excited. Something was up.

"No, he doesn't seem to suspect me at all. He even gave me a bonus," I answered. "When do I get a bonus from you?"

"If you take on the next mission I have planned for you, then you can see a little more dough in your wallet," he replied.

"A new mission?" I asked apprehensively. "I just got back from one."

"I know, but this one is super important," Mr. Zaiden replied.

"Oh yeah?" I said. "It's also important that I get a break between these missions."

"Look, it's already figured out. I have a personal jet ready to fly you to Indiana."

"Indiana?" I asked, surprised. "Seriously? That's way too

far away. What do you want from Indiana anyway? Some corn?"

Mr. Zaiden coughed, then said, "You'll have all my instructions in the briefcase on the jet tomorrow."

"Tomorrow?" I asked.

"Yes, tomorrow. You'll fly out there, get the job done, and fly back. You'll hardly be gone," Mr. Zaiden stated. "Goodbye." And he hung up.

I sighed and put my phone down. I was curious to find out why I was headed to Indiana, but I didn't want to go on another mission so soon. *I guess I'd better get ready to go, though,* I thought as I got off the couch. I went to my room to pack my gear and some clothes for the trip.

I never like packing. There were too many bad memories associated with packing. Like when my dad left us.

I was thirteen when my dad announced he was moving to Seattle and taking my brother with him. My twin sister and I begged him not to leave and to try to work out his problems with Mom, but he wouldn't listen.

What was more frustrating was that when he left, my sister and my mom didn't seem to even care. They kept telling me God would take care of us, but my dad never came home despite all their prayers.

A year later I decided to move in with my dad. Since that day, no matter how hard I tried, I couldn't forget the memory of my twin sister crying as I left. "You don't have to leave!" Sarah had said. She'd been pleading with me to stay the entire time I was packing.

"I don't have to stay either," I replied, glaring at her. "I'm tired of you and Mom nagging me to go to church and having to go to this Truth Academy school and blah blah blah."

"But Dad doesn't care about any of us," Sarah said,

standing in our room's doorway. "He hasn't even talked to us since he left."

"You don't care about me either," I'd replied, picking up my suitcase. "Now get out of my way, or I'll miss the bus."

Sarah wouldn't budge, her face stern. "Make me."

I shrugged. "Fine." I pushed my sister aside and took off at a run for the front door.

I heard Sarah's footsteps running behind me. "Please don't go!" She could barely choke out the words through her tears.

I didn't look back. I ran out the door and all the way to the bus stop. I got on the bus and headed to Seattle without saying goodbye to Sarah or my mom.

I never knew whether my decision had been a good one. I had been ahead in school and graduated from high school that year. I got my associates degree at college by the time I was sixteen, and then I got a job with Mr. Zaiden. Those were good things.

Sarah had been right about my dad, though. He didn't really care what I did or didn't do. When I asked whether I could move out after I got my job, he'd shrugged and told me it didn't matter to him. So I'd faked my age and moved into my own apartment. A week after I moved out, my dad moved to Chicago, and I hadn't heard from him since.

Ever since then, I hadn't heard from Sarah or my mom. *They never cared enough to visit anyway*, I told myself, trying to get rid of the sadness that always plagued me when I packed.

🔫

The next day before dawn, I boarded Mr. Zaiden's personal jet. As I waited for the plane ride to be over, I looked through Mr. Zaiden's instructions.

"You're headed to Fort Indiana in Indiana," the first line of the instructions read. *I've heard about this fort*, I thought. *It says this is a highly secured site that stores a lot of top-secret information, but no one knows if it really exists. How does Mr. Zaiden know about it, and what would he want from there?*

I continued reading. "Your mission is to follow the instructions on the following pages to the letter. Get the information I've asked for on the next page and then return ASAP. Zaiden."

I scanned the following instructions. Mr. Zaiden wanted me to take pictures of some documents related to some sort of security and bring them back to him. *Seems simple, except for getting access to these documents*, I thought. Mr. Zaiden had a plan, though, and if he thought it would work, then I would go for it. *I wonder why he wants pictures of these documents*, I thought as I looked out the window at the clouds.

A few hours later, we landed. One of Mr. Zaiden's contacts picked me up and drove me toward Fort Indiana. Halfway there, I switched vehicles to make tracking me more difficult and drove the rest of the way.

As I neared the fort, I pulled over to the side of the road and opened the glovebox in the car, as Mr. Zaiden had instructed. Inside were a pair of plastic gloves and a picture of a lady. She had short, red hair and wore a baseball cap. Her face shape was close to mine, and her eyes were blue like mine. Beneath her picture was the name "Lilly Jones."

After studying the picture, I hopped out of the car and went around to the trunk. I pulled out my bag and then got back in the front seat. I applied makeup to my face to look a few years older. I matched my lipstick to the color of the lipstick in the photo. Finally, I put my hair in a ponytail and tucked it into a baseball cap. I surveyed myself in the car's side mirror. I looked almost exactly like the picture of the lady.

Perfect, I thought as I started the car back up and drove the rest of the way to the fort.

🔫

The fort was surrounded by farmland. The road leading to it was long and windy. As the fort came into view, I saw a huge concrete wall, with a large metal gate, surrounding the building. There were four watchtowers, one at each corner of the wall, and there was barbed wire along the top of the wall. From the looks of it, I assumed it was electrified.

Okay, really high security, I thought as I pulled my car up to the guard shack at the gate. *I hope this disguise does the trick.* There was no one in the guard shack; however, there was a thumb scanner just outside my window for opening the gate. I pulled on the plastic gloves, then pulled a string from the side of each. The gloves suctioned to my hand so I could barely see they were there. Each finger on the gloves had a fingerprint on it to match Lilly's.

I rolled my window down and leaned out, pressing my thumb on the scanner. The words "ACCESS GRANTED" rolled across the screen, and then the gate slowly swung open. I drove through and parked in the parking spot nearest the gate. The parking lot was practically empty. I got out of the car and grabbed my purse with my special metal-detector-proof gear, then headed into the building.

Right inside the front door was a metal detector and a guard. "Place your bag here," the guard said, pointing to the scanner in front of him, "and walk through the detector." I did as I was told and was given the okay.

It was easy getting into the high-security room full of documents. The thumb scanner to enter the room worked perfectly, and I quickly found the documents Mr. Zaiden wanted. There was one guard in the room, pacing around in circles.

"Hi, Lilly," he called, waving at me.

"Hi," I replied with a nod. When his back was turned, I pulled a remote out of my purse, a disabling remote. I pointed it at the security camera facing me and clicked a few buttons. The camera's blinking lights turned off, and then I pulled out my camera. This camera was made of plastic, as small as my ring finger, and as thin as a pancake. I had snapped only a few pictures when I heard the guard's radio.

"Hey, Sam," the voice said, "camera twelve has blacked out."

"I'll check it out," the guard replied.

I stuffed my camera back into my purse and whirled around, but Sam wasn't behind me as I had feared. He was unlocking a closet at the opposite corner of the room. I pulled my camera back out of my purse, snapped a few more pictures, and then exited the room.

I exited the building with no problem and hurried over to my car. As I reached my car, another vehicle pulled up to the gate; a red-haired woman was driving.

Oh no! I thought. I jumped into the car, started it, and quickly made my way to the gate. I placed my thumb on the security pad and anxiously waited for the gate to swing open. As I waited, I heard the real Lilly yelling, "Why won't you let me in? I work here every day! Stop playing tricks on me!"

I quickly drove out the gate and back down the road, not wanting them to discover my facade.

Mr. Zaiden's instructions said to drive back to the spot I'd switched to the car and wait for a van to pick me up. I arrived at the meeting spot and switched out of my disguise as Lilly, returning my look back to Mariah.

The van's late, I thought nervously. I sat there for a few more minutes, then decided I should do something. *Might as well make my time useful*, I thought as I pulled out my camera and looked at the pictures of the documents. As I looked them over, I began to notice a theme. *These are all government security secrets. With access to these, you could do ... I don't know what all you could do. Why does Mr. Zaiden want these?*

Before I could ponder that question further, the van pulled up. I put my camera back in my purse and jumped out of the car. I jogged over to the van and jumped into the passenger seat. I set my things down by my feet as we drove off and then grabbed my seatbelt.

"Aren't we going a little fast?" I asked. I glanced over at the driver and froze.

"Nice to see you again," he replied, smiling at me.

"Jason!" I cried. "What are you doing here?"

"Giving you a ride back to your personal jet. Your driver was on a lunch break, so I offered to drive," he said, smiling.

"I'm sure that's what happened," I said suspiciously. "And the jet isn't mine."

"Oh, that's right. It belongs to your boss," Jason replied.

"How do you know that?" I asked. "And how did you know I was here? And where are we going?" We were driving in the complete opposite direction of the airport.

"One question at a time, please!" Jason said, sounding much too cheerful. "First of all, we are going back to your jet the long way. I did take time to think about the fact that some government agents could be following you, and we don't want to get caught, do we?"

I rolled my eyes and shook my head.

"Besides," he continued, "this gives me more time to chat with you."

I wanted to argue with him, but instead I kept my mouth shut. *I need to find a way out of here,* I thought, scanning the van. I didn't exactly want to jump from a moving vehicle, though, so I tried to think of other options as Jason kept talking.

"I can tell you're not paying attention, Ms. Amelia," Jason said, snapping me out of my thoughts.

"Okay, I'm listening," I replied, speaking very deliberately. "What do you want?"

"I want you to work for me," he stated. "I know about the scams that you've been helping PBPC pull off."

"I don't know what you're talking about."

"You and I both know you're a good liar."

"You can't prove anything. It's your word versus mine," I said. I couldn't deny his previous statement, but I knew my word against his would win. He was the one who'd gotten fired after all, not me.

Jason took a deep breath and began talking rapid fire. "I know. That's why I want you to work for me. It would be a quick job to get all the information we need to prove to the authorities that Patrick Brian has been stealing money from his customers, and I would pay you well."

"And send me straight to jail," I muttered without thinking. I slammed a hand over my mouth, hardly believing I had said that aloud.

"So you admit to doing wrong?" Jason asked.

"I do not! Now let me out of this car!" I shouted, pulling on the door handle, but it wouldn't open.

"Calm down! We're almost there," Jason assured me as he turned onto the street headed for the private airstrip. "Look, it's up to you. If you choose to work for me, I may be able to find a way to take out the PBPC without taking you out too, but you'd have to trust me. If you don't work for me, I happen to know some information about you that could send you straight to jail here and now."

"Are you threatening me?" I asked, glaring at him. "Why don't you just turn me in right now and save yourself the trouble."

Jason took a deep breath and gripped the steering wheel tighter. He opened his mouth to say something and then shut it again.

"Oh, I get it! You're afraid that if you turn me in, you might have to do some time too. Is that it?" I asked.

"I never said it was," he replied, pulling up next to the jet. He parked the car, and I attempted to jump out, but he stopped me. "Amelia, I would think carefully about my offer if I were you. I also happen to know that this jet isn't Mr. Brian's, and this mission you are on wasn't given to you by him," he said, motioning toward my ride home.

He's been spying on me! I thought frantically. *What is wrong with me? Why am I doing such a poor job watching my tracks?*

"Will you consider it?" he asked, resting his hand on my knee.

"Quit touching me!" I said, slapping his hand.

"Will you?" he asked again, not moving.

"Yes, now let go!" I cried, glaring at him.

He slowly released his grip and said, "Good. Here's my number. Call me when you've made up your mind." He shoved a piece of paper into my hand.

I jumped out of the car as quickly as possible and grabbed my bags. "See you later!" Jason replied, smiling.

I raced to the jet and climbed inside without looking back. "Let's go!" I yelled to the pilot as I pulled the hatch closed.

"Yes, ma'am," the pilot replied, and we started rolling toward the runway for takeoff.

I dropped into my chair and sighed. Jason's job offer didn't seem to make much sense. *I can't believe I made such a big mistake. Why haven't I been watching my back?* I thought angrily. I didn't want to think about it anymore. I leaned my chair back and closed my eyes as the jet took off.

r

I woke up a few hours later. I yawned as I pulled my chair back into a sitting position. *We still have an hour left before getting home*, I thought as I checked the time on my phone. *I guess I could look over the pictures of those documents while I wait.* I grabbed my purse and reached inside for my camera. *That's weird. I thought I put the camera in the first pocket.*

I searched throughout my purse, pulling things out frantically, but the camera wasn't there. *What happened? Did I leave it in the car?* I thought over the events of the morning. *I know I had it when I got into the van.* Then it dawned on me.

Jason had stolen my camera! I punched the arm of the chair and groaned. Why had I not noticed? "Mr. Zaiden is gonna kill me!" I muttered. "I need to get that camera back!"

r

We landed at Mr. Zaiden's private airstrip, and I bolted out of the jet and down the road as fast as I could.

"Mariah, don't hurry off so fast. Where are my pictures?" I heard Mr. Zaiden say behind me. I glanced over my shoulder and saw him stepping out of the jet's hangar and turning toward me.

"I have something urgent I need to do," I called back as I continued running. "I'll bring you the pictures later."

I ran past Mr. Zaiden's office building and dashed out of the parking lot when a car pulled in front of me, blocking my path. "Get out of my way. This is urgent!" I yelled at Mr. Zaiden as he stepped out of his car.

"Not until you give me the camera with the pictures," he said, holding out his hand.

"I can't give it to you right now," I replied. "I have to leave. There's something important—"

"You don't have the camera, do you?" Mr. Zaiden interrupted, frowning. "What happened?"

I sighed, trying to think of a way to get out of explaining that Jason had tricked me. "I don't have it right now," I said, "but I know where it is. I'm just trying to be extra cautious. Now you'd better let me go get it." I tried to walk around the car, but Mr. Zaiden grabbed my arm.

"You had better bring that camera back to me," he said, glaring at me as he tightened his grip on my arm.

"Of course I will," I replied, trying to sound reassuring. "When have I let you down?"

"I hope this isn't the first time you do," Mr. Zaiden stated. His stare was frightening; I'd never seen him so angry before.

I nodded and pulled my arm away from his grip. Then, without looking back, I ran down the street.

I took a few extra turns down some alleyways before getting back home. Inside, I pulled the paper out of my pocket and dialed the number Jason had given me.

"Hello?" Jason's voice answered cautiously.

"Hello, this is Amelia," I replied. "Where can I meet you to get that camera back?"

"So you've decided to take me up on the offer?" Jason asked.

"No, I've decided I want that camera back and now, or I'll call the cops on you!" I answered angrily.

"Okay, let's compromise. Meet me at the Italian restaurant two blocks from the PBPC building. I'll find you, and, if you answer my question, I'll give you the camera," he said.

"I already told you—" I began, but he interrupted me.

"A new question that should be easier to answer. Ten minutes. Got it?"

"Got it. I'll meet you there," I replied and hung up.

After switching my disguise to "Amelia" and checking my appearance in the mirror, I grabbed my small, high-tech Taser. It fit discreetly in my pocket, was completely silent, and held enough power to knock someone out, making a getaway easy if necessary.

I stood up and took a deep breath. *There's nothing to be nervous about,* I told myself as I headed out the door. *Just get the camera and come back. Jason is no match for you.*

I reached the rendezvous exactly on time. *I hope he's late,* I thought, glancing around. *I don't want him to know which direction I came from.*

I took a deep breath and stood up straight. *Don't be nervous,* I told myself and began walking around the building. Jason hadn't told me an exact meeting location, so I decided to look around for him.

Just as I rounded the corner of the back of the building, I felt an arm grab me around the waist and a hand clasp over my mouth. I was startled for a minute but quickly sprang into action. I kicked the person behind me, and after feeling his or her grip loosen, I pushed out of the person's grasp. I spun to face my opponent, hand on my Taser, when I recognized the person before me.

"Jason," I said, returning to a normal stance. "Fancy meeting you here."

"Nice to see you too," he said, straightening. He acted as though the past few seconds had never occurred. "Would you like to take a walk?"

"Sure," I replied, looking him over. He had no bags with him and didn't appear to be armed, but being a secret agent, I knew nothing was ever as it seemed. "Where shall we walk to?"

"Down this street," Jason replied, motioning toward the back road behind the restaurant. I waited for him to start walking and followed slightly behind him. I didn't want him sneaking up on me or anything.

"All right, let's get to the point," Jason said after we'd walked a distance from the restaurant. "You want your camera back, and I'll give it to you after you answer my question."

As I listened, I looked him over. *He'd be easy to take out, and I could just steal the camera back*, I thought, but Jason ruined that hope. "Now, I don't have the camera with me, since I assumed you would be smart enough to try to steal it without answering my question."

"Then where is it?" I asked impatiently.

"You answer my question, and I'll lead you to the location," he answered.

"How can I trust you aren't just leading me into a trap?" I asked suspiciously.

"How can I trust you're giving me a true answer to my question?" he shot back. "We'll just have to trust one another. Agreed?"

I thought about this for a moment, then replied hesitantly,

"Okay. You promise not to lead me into a trap, then I promise to answer your question."

"Promise," Jason said, holding out his hand to me. I shook it quickly and said, "Okay, what's the question?"

"Are you ready for this?" he asked dramatically. I rolled my eyes and nodded. "All right. Who owns the jet?"

I raised an eyebrow at him. "That's your question?"

He nodded and crossed his arms. "Now answer the question."

"Patrick Brian," I replied, sounding matter of fact.

"We both know that's a lie," Jason said, glaring at me. "Now tell me the real answer, or I'll have my accomplice delete all the photos from your camera."

"What makes you think I'm lying?" I asked, putting my hands on my hips. "Maybe Mr. Brian does own a jet, and you didn't know about it. You didn't work for him long, after all."

"The truth, or the pictures are deleted," he said, pulling out a phone.

It couldn't hurt Mr. Zaiden that much if I told Jason he owned the jet, I thought. *I could just tell Jason the truth, get my camera, and then take Jason out.*

"I want the answer in five, four—"

"Zaiden!" I interrupted.

"Zaiden," he repeated. "Does he have a first name?"

"You didn't ask for a full name," I replied. "Now take me to my camera, or I'll get *my* accomplices on the phone."

"Okay!" Jason said, shoving his phone back into his pocket. "Right this way."

He led the way down the street a few more blocks and turned into an alley. Pulling a key from his pocket, he unlocked a door that opened to a staircase. "It's down here," he said, motioning for me to enter.

"Gentlemen first." I pointed to the stairs and nodded in that direction.

"Okeydoke," Jason said, shrugging, and walked through the door. I followed a few steps behind.

At the bottom of the staircase, there was another door, which Jason unlocked. He walked through the doorway and straight over to a desk, which sat in the middle of an otherwise-empty room. "Here it is," he said, picking up my thin, plastic camera from the desk.

I grabbed it from his hand and looked it over. It appeared to be just fine, and I didn't find any booby traps. After checking to be sure there was still pictures on the camera, I looked around the room. There was no one else there and no other doors into the room. Not even a closet or a window.

"Looks like you didn't really have any accomplices," I said as I backed over to the door. "But I'd better be going now."

"Think about my offer!" Jason called as I bolted up the stairs. "Let me know when you decide to help me!"

I'm not going to help you at all, I thought as I slammed the outside door shut.

🔫

After meeting with Mr. Zaiden to give him the camera, I went straight home. "What a day!" I muttered as I dropped into my desk chair. I opened a writing document and recorded the events of the day, using a code language my sister and I had come up with when we were ten years old. The nice thing about it was that though the code was simple, no one (except my sister) would be able to crack it. Most people who saw me using the code thought I was writing a children's comedy story.

As I saved the events of the day, my computer phone rang. It was Mr. Zaiden.

"What do you want?" I asked. "I'm off work."

"Those pictures you gave me," his angry voice replied. "They have a virus!"

CHAPTER 3

Mr. Zaiden quickly explained that all the pictures were on the camera, but when he'd put the camera storage card into his computer, it had shut his computer down. "That's not good," I told him after he had finished ranting about viruses, my horrible job at getting these pictures, and his plans being messed up.

"What are you going to do about it?" he asked angrily.

"You should calm down and take a deep breath," I replied, hoping he would take my advice. "I said the virus wasn't good, but I didn't say it was unbeatable or anything. Let me do some research tonight, and I'll be there at seven tomorrow morning. Hopefully I'll have everything fixed before I need to go to work at the PBPC."

"Hopefully?" Mr. Zaiden asked. He didn't sound quite as enraged, but he was still obviously agitated. "You'd better fix it, or you're in trouble!"

"Okay, I will. I've got to go now so I can do some research," I said and hung up before he could reply.

I leaned back in my chair and sighed. I absently grabbed my hair and began twirling it around my finger as I thought. "Oh, I'm still in my disguise," I mumbled and trudged over to the bathroom. I removed the wig and changed into pajamas, then went to get a cup of coffee from the kitchen.

That's better, I thought as I sat down at my desk again. *Now I can concentrate.*

After reviewing the pictures and searching the web for information for a few hours, I finally found enough information to be able to remove the virus. As I printed the instructions I'd come up with, my cell phone rang. *Who's calling me at nine thirty?* I wondered as I grabbed it. Sarah was calling.

I tried to contain my surprise as I answered the phone. "Hello?"

"Um, hi, this is Sarah. Is this Rebecca?"

It felt odd to hear someone calling me by my real name. "Hi, Sarah," I replied, trying to be polite. "This is Rebecca. How are you?"

"I'm doing good. How about you?" she asked. Her voice sounded so genuine, yet it made me uncomfortable.

"I'm fine. It's been a long day, though," I answered, hoping my reply would speed up the call.

"So ... how's work?" Sarah asked rather awkwardly.

"Good," I replied and quickly changed subjects. "So why'd you call?" I slapped my hand over my mouth, regretting that blunt question.

"Because I'm your sister, and I'd like to stay in contact with you," she replied, sounding a little upset.

I rolled my eyes. *You haven't really stayed in touch before,* I thought.

Sarah took a deep breath. "Which leads me to why I called, I guess."

"What is it?"

"Would you like to meet me for lunch tomorrow

afternoon?" she asked. "I'm going to be in the area tomorrow, so I thought it would be nice to catch up with you."

"Oh, that's so ... kind of you," I said, trying to think of a good reason not to meet with her. "But, you know, I have a big project I'm working on, and I don't know for sure when my lunch break will be."

"Don't worry about that," Sarah replied. "I have a flexible schedule. Just call me when you're ready for lunch and tell me where to meet you, okay?"

"Okay," I said reluctantly. "I'll see you then."

"Bye!" Sarah said, and hung up.

I sighed. *Why does she have to show up now?* After talking about lunch, I realized I hadn't eaten dinner. I whipped up a peanut butter and jelly sandwich, quickly ate it, and then tumbled into bed, dreading the following day.

🔫

Fixing the virus turned out to be an easier job than I had thought. I was done in less than an hour.

"I'm impressed," Mr. Zaiden said after I showed him the fixed computer.

"Unfortunately, these pictures aren't very clear," I said, showing him the photos.

Mr. Zaiden surveyed the photos and waved his hand. "They're not too blurry. I should be able to decipher them."

"Good," I said, standing. "Then I'd better get going. I need to be at PBPC by nine thirty."

"Before you go, I have an offer for you," Mr. Zaiden said.

"Yes?" I asked, a little warily.

"I would like to advance your training," he began. "I have a plan that I cannot reveal to you at the moment."

"Do these pictures have anything to do with this plan?" I asked suspiciously.

"They do indeed," he answered.

"Why can't you tell me about your plan?" I asked, putting my hands on my hips. "I'm your top agent."

"I know you're my top agent," Mr. Zaiden said impatiently, "but if I tell anyone my plans before they're finalized, it could jeopardize the entire thing. Do you understand?" I nodded, and he continued. "Now, about that training. I think you're ready to become an assassin."

"A what?" I asked, not believing what I'd just heard.

"An assassin," he stated calmly.

My mouth dropped open for a second before I replied, "No thanks. I'm not killing anyone."

"Of course you'll go through a lot of training, and you won't even go on any kind of mission until you're totally comfortable."

"Mr. Zaiden," I replied coldly, "I will never be your assassin. Train someone else—train Lisa—but you aren't training me."

"But Mariah, think of all the opportunities this will give you. This job will raise your salary substantially, and you'll be able to travel around the world."

I took a deep breath to calm my emotions. "Mr. Zaiden," I said slowly, "thank you for the offer, but I could never be an assassin."

"I think you will change your mind," Mr. Zaiden replied calmly. "Think it over. You're my only agent that would even fit the job, but it's up to you. Now you'd better get going, or you'll be late to work."

The rest of the morning was an uneventful blur as my mind replayed Mr. Zaiden's offer. I was still shocked. I hadn't seen it coming. *Why can't things just stay the way they've always been? That's how I've always liked it*, I thought.

Before I knew it, it was lunchtime. I walked out the door of the office building and slowly let it close. *I guess I have to call Sarah now*, I thought as I reluctantly pulled my cellphone out of my purse.

Sarah answered promptly. "Hello!" she said cheerfully.

"Hi, Sarah," I replied. "I'm on my lunch break now. Were you still planning to meet me for lunch, or have you already eaten?"

"Oh, no, I haven't eaten yet. I've been waiting. Do you want to meet me at the little sandwich place downtown?" she asked.

I sighed. "Sure. That sounds great. I'll be there in twenty minutes. Bye." *I'd better get moving*, I thought as I hurried back to my apartment. *That sandwich shop is four miles from here.*

After quickly stopping at my apartment to take off my wig and switch purses, I headed to the sandwich shop, arriving at the same time as Sarah.

"Rebecca!" Sarah cried as she got out of her car. She ran over to me and gave me a big hug. I hugged her back, trying to calm my breathing down from running part of the way here. "It's so nice to see you again," Sarah said after releasing me. "You look so much older."

"So do you," I replied. Sarah was still my complete identical. Her wavy brown hair came down to her midback like mine. Her blue eyes were as bright as ever. Her skin color was still pale like mine, but she definitely looked more like an adult than a teenager, even though she was only eighteen. The only thing about the two of us that wasn't identical was our height, since she was five foot eight and I was barely an inch taller.

Sarah looked at me quizzically for a moment.

"What's wrong?" I asked.

"Uh, well, um, your eyebrows are, um ..." Sarah bit her lip and quit speaking.

"Oh!" I exclaimed, realizing I'd forgotten about my blonde eyebrows. "I dyed my eyebrows for a drama I was in a while ago, and it hasn't washed out yet," I lied, giggling nervously.

Sarah seemed to believe me as she nodded and giggled, and we went into the sandwich shop. After ordering our lunch, we began catching up. Sarah's sweet personality was so familiar, putting me at ease. I practically forgot about all my secret-agent worries until Sarah asked about work.

"So what exactly do you do at work?" Sarah asked, looking at me expectantly.

I took a bite of my sandwich before replying, "Well, I fix things. I mostly work on the computers."

"And you're working at the power company, right?" she asked.

"Yes," I answered. Something about that question just seemed off. *She already knew that. Why would she ask?* I thought suspiciously.

I cleared my throat and changed the subject. "Are you going to college now?"

"No, I'm actually working," she replied, smiling.

"Really?" I asked, wide eyed. "What do you do?"

"I work for Truth Academy," she answered. "I'm a teacher."

"Don't you have to be, like, twenty-one to be a teacher?" I asked.

"No." She finished her sandwich and wiped her hands on her napkin.

"Did you actually go to college?" I asked awkwardly.

"Yes, I did," Sarah answered. "Truth Academy has a program that allows you to graduate from college and high school at the same time. I got done a little early, when I was seventeen, and this year I was able to start teaching."

"So you enjoy it then," I said, leaning on my elbow.

"I love it!" she said, then cleared her throat. "What about you? Do you enjoy your work?"

"Totally," I replied.

"Good," she said. After an awkward silence, she continued, "So I'm actually going to be in the area for a while."

"Wait, don't you have to teach?" I asked. "I mean, it is fall." *Don't tell me we have to meet for lunch again*, I wanted to say but didn't.

"Not at the moment. Anyways, I thought maybe we could meet for lunch again sometime," she said, shrugging.

"Possibly," I replied as a sinking feeling came over me. I checked the time on my phone. "I need to get back to work." I stood up to leave.

"Do you need a ride?" Sarah asked, standing. "I can drive you."

"No, it's all right. It's not too far from here," I assured her quickly. "But I'd better leave now."

"Well, it was great catching up with you," she said, giving me a hug before I left.

"Bye," I replied and hurried out the door.

                                                                                 ☞

The next week went by without any problems, but Mr. Zaiden's and Jason's job offers were on my mind constantly. I didn't want to become an assassin, but I didn't really want to turn on Mr. Zaiden after all the training he'd given me. *Just say no to both*, I kept on telling myself, but I knew I wouldn't be able to do that.

That Thursday, after a long morning of working on some training techniques with my coworkers, I was packing my things to head home when Mr. Zaiden appeared in my office doorway.

"Mariah, do you have a minute?"

"Only one," I replied as I finished putting my equipment in my pack.

"I've been watching your training, and you've been doing very well," he said. "Now, I think you're ready for that job I offered you. If you'd just reconsider—"

"I gave you an answer, and it's final. I don't want to have the guilt of assassination on my head," I replied shortly.

He sighed. "I wish you'd reconsider. You're the best person for the job."

"But you were an assassin, weren't you?" I asked. "Don't you feel guilty?"

"One thing you learn as an assassin is to never feel guilty," he replied, his cold stare making me shiver. "So think my offer over."

I left the building in a hurry and ran home. As I changed clothes and wigs to go to work at the PBPC, my mind raced, thinking about what Mr. Zaiden had said. *It sounded like a threat to me. But he would never threaten me. I'm his best agent!* I argued with myself.

My day at the PBPC didn't go well. Mr. Brian was clearly

frustrated with me. "You're not doing a very good job. Everything is looking sloppy."

"I'm sorry," I mumbled as I redid my work. "I just have a lot on my mind today."

Due to having to redo so much, I was late getting off work. The sun was setting just as I stepped outside the office door. "Great," I mumbled as I began walking home. I hated walking home in the dark, especially in this shady part of the city. Times like this made me wish I owned a car, but I'd never seen the need since anytime either boss needed me to travel, he always provided the ride.

As I stepped onto the sidewalk just outside the PBPC property, someone jumped out in front of me. I was startled and jumped backward but then regained my composure. "Excuse me," I said as calmly as possible. "I believe I was walking down this sidewalk."

"I think so," a man replied. It was Jason.

"Could you be so kind as to let me continue?" I asked, exasperated.

"When we're done talking," he replied. "Would you like me to walk you home or to my office?"

"Neither," I answered. "I'm tired of you getting in my way." I tried to continue walking down the street, but he blocked me.

"You'll come to my office then," he said, poking a gun in my back.

Realizing I'd left my gun at home, I inwardly scolded myself. *That's such a rookie mistake. Get your act together, girl!* Rolling my eyes, I said, "Fine. I'll come."

Jason led me down the street and through some alleys. We ended up at the same building where I'd met him to get my camera. "Please walk down the stairs," he said after opening the door. I glared at him but continued down the stairs since he held the gun.

Jason followed right behind me, and after reaching the bottom of the stairs, he pointed me to a folding chair in the middle of the room.

"What do you want?" I asked, folding my arms as I sat down.

"I want you to answer a few questions. That's all," he said, shrugging. "Are you ready for this?"

"Ready for what? I know how to answer a question," I said while thinking, *I also know how to bluff.*

"First off, about that Zaiden dude," Jason said as he began pacing back and forth in front of me. "Did you know he has a history?"

"Doesn't everyone have a history?" I shot back.

"I mean a criminal record kind of history," he said, rolling his eyes.

I shrugged. "As I said, doesn't everyone?"

"Amelia, let's quit this game. I'll just tell you what I've learned," Jason said, stooping down to eye level. "I checked into that airplane to see who owned it. The owner goes by the name of Nathaniel Baker, so I checked into that name, but I didn't really get any leads there."

Smart thinking on his part, I thought. *And bad on mine. I shouldn't have let him get near that jet.*

"So I checked into the last name Zaiden." Jason stood up and began pacing again. "There was more than one, but after a lot of work, I narrowed my options down to two men— one Zaiden is a retired karate teacher who lives in Seattle. The other is a man on the wanted list for assassinating a government official ten years ago, but he's never been found, and no one knows what he looks like."

My eyes grew wide as I heard the description of these two men. Jason turned to face me and said, "I have a feeling that one of these two men is the man you work for."

I glared at him. "I have a feeling you need to do some more homework."

"If you could see your own face," Jason said as he struggled to keep from smiling, "you would know that one of those two men is your boss."

I froze. I hadn't kept the emotion from my face. *What's wrong with me?* I inwardly screamed. *Why do I keep messing up?* I happened to know that Mr. Zaiden had taught karate for a few years, since it was a hobby of his, but he had given it up after he started training agents to work for him. Both of the men Jason had described were my boss, and I couldn't tell him that it was one or the other.

"So which guy is your boss?" Jason asked. I looked away and began scanning the room, trying to think of a way to escape.

"Amelia," Jason said, waving his hand in front of my face. "Let's answer this question so we can get on to the next one."

"The next one?" I cried. "Isn't one enough?"

"Oh, no way!" Jason said, waving his hand. "I've got three!" His nonchalant attitude was almost scary.

"Look, I'm not going to tell you who my boss is."

"Okay, we'll skip that question and come back to it," Jason said. "Question number two: would you please help me stop Mr. Brian from stealing people's money and catch this Zaiden assassin dude?"

"It's so kind of you to say 'please,'" I answered sarcastically.

"So it's a yes?" Jason asked, grinning at me excitedly. He almost reminded me of a seven-year-old with all his enthusiasm.

"Ah, no," I replied. "I have my loyalties." Jason was getting on my nerves more and more.

"Aren't you loyal to your friends and family? Mr. Brian is stealing money from people, and that includes them. Plus, Zaiden is a dangerous assassin who could hurt you or your family or friends!" Jason said earnestly.

"I don't have friends," I replied, "and I don't work for an assassin." I worked harder to keep my face emotionless this time.

"Don't avoid my question," he said, glaring at me.

"But don't you have your loyalties?" I retorted. "The PBPC supplies power to all of Seattle and most of Washington, Oregon, and California. Do you want three states to lose power? Do you want your city to lose power?"

"That won't happen," Jason said. "We would be replacing Mr. Brian with a more honest and responsible person."

"Hold on. Who is 'we'?" I said. "Who are you working for?"

"Um, well ... I'm sort of self-employed, but I have connections," Jason replied, avoiding the answer. "Anyway, it's you who needs to decide where your loyalties lie. Do they lie with a cheat and a murderer? Because if so, you're living with a lot of uncertainty."

"Yeah, right," I replied. "My bosses have been loyal to me."

"For how long? Only for as long as you do what they need you to do. When you quit doing what they want, you're out," Jason stated, crossing his arms.

I tried to think of a reply, but I couldn't. He was probably right. I'd learned that I couldn't trust anyone. *If I can't trust Mr. Brian and Mr. Zaiden, then I can't trust Jason either,* I thought.

"So what do you say?" Jason asked.

I glared at him and replied, "Nope."

"Why not?" he asked, looking genuinely disappointed.

"Why should I trust a stranger?" I asked.

"Why should you trust a cheat and a murderer?" Jason retorted.

I sighed in frustration. *Does he have to answer everything I say with a question?* This guy wasn't giving up.

"I'll even throw some money into the deal," Jason said slyly.

"Oh yeah? How much?" I wondered aloud.

"Sixty thousand dollars," Jason replied, grinning. "More than enough for the job."

I wanted to say no, but $60,000 was a lot ... a lot more than any single job I'd ever done for Zaiden or Brian. *It's not worth the risk,* part of me thought. *But that's some serious money,* the other part of me thought. *Why turn it down?*

I thought hard. Finally, I asked, "Can we compromise? I'll give you information as long as that's all I have to do."

Jason thought for a moment, then nodded. "All right, it's a deal ... for now."

"For now?" I asked suspiciously.

"For now. Eventually you're gonna have to choose sides," he answered.

Or not, I thought. "So what's your third question?" I asked.

"What?" Jason asked, looking confused.

"You said you had three questions for me," I replied.

"Oh, right," Jason said, nodding. He walked over to his desk and opened a drawer. "My third question was supposed to wait until I'd convinced you to help me." He pulled a box out of the drawer. "So now that we've got that out of the way, would you like a doughnut?" He pulled out a powdered doughnut from the box and offered it to me.

My jaw dropped. *Is he serious? This guy's weird,* I thought.

"No thanks," I answered, not wanting to risk eating a poisoned doughnut.

"Are you sure?" he asked. "There are three kinds in this box." He waved the box excitedly.

"I'm sure," I replied. "Can I go home now?"

He took a bite of the doughnut and smiled. "Mmm, I love a good doughnut. And yes, you can go home. Just close the door as you leave."

I stared at him suspiciously. "Okay," I said, standing slowly and backing toward the stairs. "No following me."

"Okeydoke," he replied as he continued eating.

I ran out of the building and carefully surveyed the area, making sure no one was following me or ready to jump out at me. After I felt a little more confident that Jason was still in his office, I took off down the street and headed home as fast as possible.

Arriving at home, I ran inside and slammed the door shut. Sighing, I sat down and tugged my wig off my head. *I'm such a traitor,* I thought angrily as I unpinned my hair.

I'm not a traitor. I'm just being smart, I argued with myself. *I worked for Zaiden first. But Zaiden's getting creepy with his whole assassin thing. But I don't care that he was an assassin. I just don't want to be one. But what if Jason is right? What if Mr. Zaiden will only be loyal to me until I don't do as he asks?*

I tossed my wig and bobby pins onto the couch and crawled into bed without changing into pajamas. *Why did Jason have to complicate an already-complicated job?* I thought before drifting off to sleep.

CHAPTER 4

The next week flew by quickly. On Monday, after a long day's work at PBPC, Mr. Brian gave me some vacation days. "You have Tuesday through Sunday off," he told me as I got ready to leave.

"Well, thank you, sir," I replied, nodding.

"I'm impressed by your work, Amelia. You always deliver a top-quality job," Mr. Brian said, clasping his hands. "I don't know what we'd do without you."

"Thank you, sir. I'll see you next week." With a wave I walked out of the building. Just as I exited, I got a call from Mr. Zaiden. I pressed the answer button on my earphone and said, "This is Mariah."

"This is Zaiden. Meet me at my office. I have some very important news for you." His voice sounded serious, making me nervous. "What is your ETA?"

"Leaving PBPC. Around thirty minutes," I answered, picking up my pace.

"Over and out," Mr. Zaiden said and hung up.

I hurried home, switched into my red wig, and hurried back out the door. Thirty minutes later, I ran into Mr. Zaiden's office.

"Good evening," Mr. Zaiden said as I entered the room. "Take a seat."

I sat down and asked, "What's up?"

"I think it's time to step up our game with the power company. You've been doing a lot of research and learning a lot working for Brian. I think it's time to start tearing down the company," Mr. Zaiden explained.

"I'm assuming you want to take over the power company for yourself?" I asked.

"You're catching on," Mr. Zaiden answered with a nod. "It will be a great help to own that power company. Now, while you're on your break, I'll need you to do some work for me."

"Hold it! How did you know I was on break?" I asked, leaning forward in my chair.

"I'm your boss. I know things," Mr. Zaiden replied.

I shook my head. *I'm going to have to keep a closer eye on things,* I thought. *I can't have Mr. Zaiden knowing my every move.*

"So let's meet here tomorrow afternoon at one o'clock and discuss our plan," Mr. Zaiden continued.

"All right." I stood up and turned to leave, saying, "I'll be here."

The next morning I woke up, prepared to go to work, when I realized I didn't have to be anywhere until noon. "Man, I could have slept in," I mumbled after my realization. But I was already wide awake, so I stayed up.

After eating breakfast, I sat down to read a magazine and kill time when my phone rang.

"Hey, Rebecca!" my sister's cheerful voice sang after I answered. "How are you this morning?"

"Good since I don't have to work this morning," I replied.

"Perfect!" Sarah said excitedly, and I cringed. "Since you aren't busy, could I stop by your place to visit?"

"Uh, well, I don't ... um ..." I thought frantically, not wanting Sarah to know where I lived. That would be a dangerous move. "Why don't we meet at the park? It's a nice day out, and it's not raining."

"That's a good idea. I'll meet you there. What time?" she asked.

"How about nine thirty?" I suggested.

"That works for me. See you then!" she said and hung up.

I sighed and stood up with a yawn. "I guess there's no being lazy for me," I muttered as I started getting ready for the day.

During my walk to the park, I began wondering why Sarah was in town. *It's odd that she'd just show up like that, especially since we haven't talked in so long,* I thought, but then I told myself there was no reason to suspect her of something. *That's not like Sarah. She'd never spy on me. Quit overthinking everything.*

I reached the park before Sarah did, so I sat on a bench to wait. The park was small, only covering half a block, but it was quite elegant, having a small, stone fountain in the middle surrounded by newly planted maple trees. In the far corner of the park was a green play set with a few toddlers on it, reminding me of the park my family used to go to when I was little. I watched the kids play for a few minutes, smiling sadly as I remembered all the good times our family had enjoyed before everything had gone wrong. *No time for being sad, though,* I told myself as I turned away. *You have too much to do to be distracted.*

I checked my watch. 9:42. *Sarah's late. That's weird. She hates being late.* I glanced around nervously, wondering where she was.

Just then I heard Sarah call, "Rebecca!" I turned around to see her skipping toward me from the opposite end of the park, waving at me. I waved back and shook my head, smiling. Sarah was eighteen and still skipping around like a little girl. *I wish I was still a little girl,* I thought as I walked over to meet her.

"So sorry I'm late," Sarah apologized. "I got lost trying to find the park. I hope you weren't waiting long." She looked eagerly at me.

"Oh, it's not a problem," I said with a wave.

"Good," Sarah replied cheerfully, linking her arm in mine. "Why don't we walk around the park? You were right about it being a lovely day."

"Why not?" I agreed as she pulled me with her.

We visited as we walked, and I found myself enjoying the time. Sarah had an endless supply of questions, but so did I. Before I knew it, we'd been visiting for almost an hour.

"Oh, dear," I said, looking up from my watch. "Sarah, I've got to go. I'm meeting with my boss."

"Oh, all right," Sarah said with a dramatic sigh. "We'll have to get together another time."

"That'd be fine," I said, smiling.

"Would you like to go to church with me this Sabbath?" Sarah asked politely. I shook my head. "Why not?" she asked.

"I'm busy this weekend," I replied, staring at the ground. That wasn't exactly the whole truth, but I decided I'd make it the truth.

"Well, some other time then," Sarah said, then changed the subject. "So why are you meeting with your boss?"

"He's got some plans he needs help with. I'm one of his top employees, you know," I replied as I walked with Sarah to her car.

"I didn't know," she said, raising an eyebrow at me. "I thought you were just the tech person."

"Oh, well, yeah," I answered awkwardly, realizing she didn't know about Mr. Zaiden. "I work two jobs."

"Really? No wonder you're so busy!" Sarah exclaimed.

"Yeah, well, I'm hoping that I won't have to work two jobs soon. It's been a little stressful with timing and the competition and all," I said, then froze, realizing what I'd just said.

"Timing? Competition? What exactly is your second job?" Sarah asked, her eyes expressing concern.

"Oh, it's just a ... I, uh, train people for martial arts competitions, and my schedule for training and working at the PBPC isn't always lined up," I lied and smiled. "Which is why I need to meet with my boss so we can try to work out a better schedule."

Sarah raised an eyebrow at me. She obviously wasn't buying it. "Is everything really okay?" she asked. "If you're in trouble ..."

"I'm not in trouble. Don't you believe me?" I asked, hoping to guilt her so she wouldn't notice my bluff.

"I believe you were telling the truth about being stressed out, which is why I'm concerned," Sarah replied. "Don't let your boss take advantage of you."

"That won't happen," I assured her. "But I'd better get going."

"All right, bye," Sarah said, giving me a hug. "I'll be praying for you."

"Okay, thanks. Bye," I replied awkwardly and watched her get into her car and drive away. Something about what she had said reminded me of what Jason had said. *Why are they both concerned about my bosses? I can take care of myself*, I thought angrily as I stomped on home.

Later that afternoon, I rushed into Mr. Zaiden's office and plopped down in the chair across from him. I was a little late, but he didn't seem to notice.

"Glad you're here, Mariah," Mr. Zaiden said without even a glance at me. He sat at his computer and stared intently at whatever was on the screen.

"Are you busy?" I asked, not wanting to waste time when I had the day off.

"No, no, no," he replied, still not looking at me. "I'm just finishing this up." He sat silently for a minute, then clicked a few buttons on his computer before turning to face me. "All right, let's get to it."

"We're talking about plans, right?" I asked.

"Correct, but first I have a different plan I need to tell you," he said, smiling at me.

"Don't tell me I need to go on another mission," I moaned, slumping in my chair.

"Don't try to assume things when I haven't told you anything," Mr. Zaiden replied, still smiling. The look on his face piqued my interest.

"So what is it?"

"I'm promoting you to my new assistant," he announced excitedly.

"Seriously?" I exclaimed, almost jumping out of my chair.

"Seriously," Mr. Zaiden assured me. "You deserve a promotion. After all, you're my best agent."

"Thanks!" I replied. I couldn't stop myself from grinning. This was awesome.

"But remember to keep my other offer in mind," Mr. Zaiden reminded me, and my smile quickly faded. "Now let's get to talking about Brian's company. I need you to get some information for me. I want you to put all that research to good use and go undercover this week to get some hard evidence."

Now this is like it, I thought as we went over the details of the mission. *Some great action and time to practice my acting skills. This is why I love being a double agent.* Then I remembered that I also worked for Jason now. *Make that a triple agent.*

"Well, I think you've got your work cut out for you," Mr. Zaiden said as I stood up to leave.

"Definitely, but it'll be fun," I said, opening the office door.

"I'll see you in two days," he replied.

I waved, then walked down the stairs and out the building. As I exited Mr. Zaiden's property, my phone rang. I walked around the bend so Mr. Zaiden couldn't see me and answered the phone. "Hello?"

"This is Jason," came the reply. "Meet me in the usual spot in thirty minutes."

"Why? Wait. What usual spot?" I asked, but then he hung up. "Oh brother," I muttered as I put my phone back into my bag. "I guess I still don't have the day off."

I hurried home and changed into my "Amelia" costume. Since Jason hadn't told me where the "usual spot" was, I decided he must have meant his office and took off in that direction. Jason met up with me before I arrived.

"Hello! It's a nice day, isn't it?" he said cheerfully as I approached.

I smiled and replied, "Yes, it is." Jason's cheerfulness was almost comical compared to the serious personalities of my other bosses.

"Follow me. We're taking a scenic route," Jason said, looping his arm through mine.

"Don't do that," I said, jerking my arm away from him.

"Don't you want to blend in?" he asked, putting his arm back where it had been.

I rolled my eyes but didn't say anything. He was right; there were lots of people around, and we would fit in better acting like friends instead of enemies.

Jason's "scenic" route took us through several alleys and back roads, entering the main road several times as well. "What's with the long route?" I asked as we neared his office.

"Security," he replied. We walked over to his office, and after he unlocked the door, I hurried down the stairs as he relocked the door.

"So what's this meeting about?" I asked impatiently. "It had better be short because I have things to do today."

"I'm sure you do. You're a busy person," Jason said with a smirk.

"Then do hurry up," I replied, glaring at him.

"I want you to find a little info for me," Jason said. I started to protest, but he shook his head. "We agreed that you would just find info for me and nothing more, remember? So here's your first assignment."

I sighed. "Okay, fine. What is it?"

"It's simple. I just need you to get me some solid proof that Patrick Brian has been stealing money from his customers. Got it?" he asked, looking expectantly at me.

"That is super descriptive," I replied sarcastically. "Would you like to be more specific? You know, I could just as easily make up fake evidence for you."

"Glad you mentioned that, but I think you know what to do," Jason said. His solid gaze made me feel nervous. *He couldn't possibly know Mr. Zaiden asked me to get the same information, could he?* I wondered.

I put on a confident expression and said, "All right, I guess I know what to do. When do you want this information by?"

"In three days."

"Good. That'll give you plenty of time to do some planning on how I'm getting into the building without it being awkward," I said, nodding triumphantly.

"Why would it be awkward?" Jason asked, raising an eyebrow. "You work there."

"I have the week off," I replied.

"Oh ... well then, I do need to work on changing my plan," Jason said, resting his finger thoughtfully on his chin. "That shouldn't be a problem, though," he said confidently after a moment. "You get ready to do some snooping. You know, do whatever research you need to do. I'll get a plan ready."

"All right. Do you want me back here in three days?" I asked, getting ready to leave.

"Yes. Make sure you come here early," Jason said quickly before I could leave. "I have some special equipment I need you to use."

"I have my own equipment. I don't need yours," I replied

coldly. *His equipment is probably nothing compared to mine anyway,* I thought.

"Well, come early anyway. You can look my equipment over and see if you like any of it," Jason replied. "See you later!" He waved as I ran up the stairs. He seemed so calm and cheerful; he made me wish I wasn't so overwhelmed so I could enjoy my job more.

You don't have to be like him, though, my brain argued with itself. *He's kind of weird anyway.*

I walked slowly back toward my apartment, taking another long route home. *Better safe than sorry,* I told myself, trying to keep from feeling overwhelmed. *I just need to do a little research and calm down. I love my job; I'm just a little off my game.*

I wondered for a minute why I was off my game. *Everything was fine until Jason messed it up ... It's Jason's fault. I just need to find a way to get him out of my life,* I decided. Suddenly Mr. Zaiden's offer popped into my mind, but I shooed that away. *I will not assassinate anyone, not even Jason. Ever.*

I stomped up to my apartment and unlocked the door. I stepped inside and slammed it shut. "Why is everything so confusing?" I whispered, locking the door.

*

Research went quickly and easily. Working for the PBPC as a tech made it easy to get into the computer system remotely. I finished research by the time both Jason and Mr. Zaiden needed it done, which happened to be the same day, Friday. *Strange coincidence,* I wondered as I printed the necessary info and put it in my bag.

First, I headed over to Jason's office at five thirty a.m.

"He'd better be here," I grumbled as I stomped down the street. "Five thirty is way too early."

As I rounded the corner into the alley leading to his office, I saw someone running out the opposite end of the alley—a person who had wavy brown hair and was about my height.

"Sarah?" I called, but the person didn't answer. I stood still for a minute, stunned. Finally, I shook my head. *That couldn't have been Sarah*, I told myself as I walked over to Jason's office door. *I didn't see the person's face anyway. It couldn't have been her.*

I knocked loudly on Jason's door and waited. I heard what sounded like a bunch of mice being attacked by metal chairs. *What in the world is going on?* I wondered.

I turned the doorknob to see if it would open. The door wasn't locked, but something was keeping it shut. I looked around the door for another lock, but I couldn't find one. *Weird*, I thought as I ran my hand over the door. I knocked again, but the loud noises downstairs continued. *He probably can't hear with that racket. Maybe I should break in.*

I examined the door again and finally found what I was looking for—an invisible keypad! Below the handle was a thin piece of glass, only a few inches wide and maybe one inch long. I pulled my makeup bag out of my purse and, after grabbing my blush and a makeup brush, dusted the piece of glass. There was a pattern of fingerprints across the glass. I tapped the glass in the order in which the fingerprints had appeared, and after a few more attempts of trying different patterns, the door unlocked.

"Awesome!" I whispered, quite satisfied with my accomplishment.

I ran down the stairs to find Jason pushing his desk, which made quite a ruckus. His desk was obviously heavy, and he looked like he'd run a marathon. "Hey!" I called loudly.

"Oh, hey, what are you doing back already?" he grunted without looking at me, still pushing the desk.

"What do you mean, 'back already'? It's Friday! And it's five forty. I'm a little late," I replied, still yelling over the scraping of the desk.

Jason stopped, slid down to the floor, and wiped the sweat off his face. "But I thought you said ..." He glanced over at me and quit speaking. "Oh, right! It's Friday. Hello, Amelia. Um, how'd you get in? Did I leave the door unlocked?"

I eyed him suspiciously. He was obviously trying to cover for something or maybe someone. "The door wasn't exactly unlocked, but it wasn't a problem," I replied. "Anyways, let's make this fast. I don't really have time to—"

"Hey, you'll be grateful you took time to see this equipment," Jason interrupted as he pulled a large cardboard box out from the corner of the room. He pushed the box up to my feet, then stood up straight. "This, my friend, is top-quality, never-seen-before, awesomely amazingly cool—"

"Get to the point!" I urged.

"Oh, right," Jason said, giving me a thumbs-up. "This equipment is stuff you've never seen before, and it's awesome. Trust me—I know."

"How do you know whether I've seen it or not?" I asked, but I still felt curious, wanting to see inside.

"I helped invent some of it, but that's top-secret info," Jason replied, crossing his arms triumphantly. "Go ahead and take a look."

I opened the box to find it full of equipment, way too much for one agent alone. "I wouldn't be able to carry all this stuff," I said as I pulled what looked like a normal wallet out of the box.

"You won't carry all of it at once," Jason assured me.

"You'll just take what you need for each mission. What's way cool about this stuff is that it's undetectable. You can walk through any metal detector and not be found."

I quit examining the wallet to look inside the box again. "Um, even that?" I asked, pointing to a sheet of metal.

"Well, not that, but everything else," Jason replied, grinning sheepishly. "The metal is for fixing my desk." He pulled the sheet out and took it to the other side of his desk. "Go ahead and look through all that stuff. You've got time."

I finally figured out that the wallet was actually a mini computer. "That's pretty cool," I admitted.

"I know, right? I wish I'd thought of that. My inventor buddy, Matt, made that," Jason said from under his desk.

I pulled out more gadgets: earring earpieces, a tracking device ring, a notebook that took pictures and copied them onto the pages, climbing gear disguised as a pair of shoes, and a watch with knockout gas inside.

"Is the knockout gas a good idea if there's no protection for the person wearing the watch?" I asked, as I handed the watch to Jason.

"Yeah, I thought of that, too, while I was making it," Jason said, examining the watch. "I'm still working out the bugs on this one, so don't take it with you."

I nodded and continued looking through the box. There were so many gadgets; I knew I wouldn't have time to look at them all. "So what do you want me to bring along on this mission?" I asked, still rummaging through the box.

"Wear the earring earpieces. That way we can stay in contact," Jason began.

Suddenly, I realized I now had two bosses who would be trying to walk me through this break-in. After a little contemplation, I decided it would be best to tell Jason instead of Mr. Zaiden. "We have a problem," I said reluctantly. "You're not the only one I'll need to stay in contact with."

"Hmm, that is a problem," Jason said thoughtfully. "Okay, so is this other person wanting you to get the same info?"

I shrugged but didn't answer.

"Okay, I'll take it as a yes," Jason continued. "So you wear the earrings. I'll set them up so that I'll hear everything you say but you won't hear me. Does that work with you?"

"I suppose," I replied hesitantly. The idea of Jason hearing everything I said without me hearing him wasn't my first choice, but I decided I would go with it, because I needed him to trust me.

After getting all the equipment I could possibly want or need, I ran home, switched my costume to "Mariah," and ran to Mr. Zaiden's office. I made sure to leave all my new equipment behind at my house, not wanting Jason to eavesdrop on any conversations and not wanting Mr. Zaiden to know about this equipment. *At least the new stuff gives me the advantage over Mr. Zaiden,* I thought as I ran up the stairs to his office. *This could turn the tables for me.*

"Are you ready for this assignment?" Mr. Zaiden asked. He was waiting for me at the top of the stairs.

"Totally ready!" I replied, excitement bubbling in me. I loved the thrill of a new assignment.

"Then let's review our plan," Mr. Zaiden said, and I followed him into his office.

Two hours later I stood outside the PBPC office building, geared up and ready to go.

"Coms check," I said quietly as I walked up to the front door.

"Check, check," Mr. Zaiden's voice blasted into my ears.

"Wow! Definitely loud and clear," I replied. "Can you turn yourself down a little? I don't want people to overhear us."

"I'll do that," came his loud reply.

I opened the door and stood face-to-face with a security guard. "Please walk through this doorway and place your purse in this tray," the security guard said with a yawn. He'd obviously been working a while.

I placed my purse in the tray and took a deep breath. *I hope Jason told the truth about his equipment being undetectable*, I thought worriedly. I stepped through the metal detector.

"All clear. Go on ahead," the security guard said, handing me my purse.

"Thanks," I replied and kept on walking. I sighed with relief. *That was easy*, I thought as I continued down the hall.

"You're in?" Mr. Zaiden asked, his voice much quieter now.

"Yup, I'm in," I replied quietly. I hoped Jason was truly listening so he could activate my equipment remotely. "I'm headed to Brian's office," I said, pushing a button on my new purse. Jason had promised it would send an electronic wave to the security cameras and cause them to blink, allowing me just enough time to get by undetected. I hoped Jason's equipment was flawless.

I got to Brian's office and took out my lockpick. I knew Mr. Brian was speaking at a conference in Los Angeles, so I didn't have to worry about running into him. I unlocked the door and slipped inside.

"I'm in," I whispered softly as I pressed a button on my watch, notifying Jason to loop the camera's image.

"Disable the cameras," Mr. Zaiden said.

Already done, I thought triumphantly.

I walked over to the file cabinet, unlocked it with my lockpick, and rummaged quickly through the files.

"Did you disable the cameras?" Mr. Zaiden's voice rang into my ears, sounding worried.

"Yes," I replied. "I'm getting into the files now." I pulled out the file I was looking for and shut the cabinet. "Okay, I've found it," I said. I pulled a dusting cloth from my purse and dusted off the cabinet to remove my fingerprints. After relocking the door and dusting off the handle, I slipped out of the office door and began walking back down the hall.

"I'm making my exit," I said softly into my earpiece.

"Good work," Mr. Zaiden replied.

As I neared the front doors, I saw one of my coworkers coming in. "Oh no! Problem," I whispered as I slipped into the women's restroom.

"Now what?" Mr. Zaiden asked.

"My coworker just entered the building. If she spots me, I'm toast," I replied.

"Where are you now?" Mr. Zaiden asked.

"The bathroom," I replied awkwardly.

"Exit through the window," he suggested.

"What about the security guard?" I asked. "He'll notice that I never left the building."

My watch beeped. I looked down to see a message from Jason on the screen. "She'll be going to her office," it read. "Wait thirty sec, then head to the door. She should be gone by then."

"Never mind," I said into my earpiece. "I think I've figured it out."

"You'd better have," Mr. Zaiden growled.

I peeked out the bathroom door and, seeing that the coast was clear, walked briskly down the hall toward the door.

"Walk back through the detector," the guard said.

I walked quickly through, was given the go-ahead, and walked out the door.

After walking down the street a few blocks, I quietly asked, "Where do I meet you?"

"Meet me on Third Street," came Mr. Zaiden's reply.

"Copy that," I said as I darted into a secondhand store. I meandered over to the clothes racks and pretended to look at the dresses. Pushing my purse in between the clothes, I pulled the notebook camera out of my purse along with the file. I flipped quickly through the file, taking a picture of each page, then slipped the notebook and file back into my purse. After looking through dresses a little longer, I walked back out the door and headed to Third Street.

I arrived at the rendezvous and waited for Mr. Zaiden. A few minutes later, I saw him walking toward me on the opposite side of the street. He nodded toward the crosswalk, so I headed in that direction. I grabbed the file out of my purse and held it firmly as I crossed the street. I met Mr. Zaiden halfway in the crosswalk and handed off the file. After reaching the other side of the street, I spoke into my earpiece. "Got it?"

"Got it," Mr. Zaiden replied, smiling at me. "Good work." With that he turned around and walked away.

I pulled my earpieces out of my ears and shoved them into my purse. Using my watch, I messaged Jason, asking him whether I should come to his office.

"Yes. Come to my office. Let's look over the file," his message said.

🔫

Jason stood outside his door, waiting for me. "Welcome!" he said cheerfully as he opened the door. I hurried down the stairs as he followed.

Jason began to say something, but I shushed him. I pulled the earpieces from my purse and mouthed, "What do we do with these?"

Jason gave me a thumbs-up, grabbed the earpieces from me, and took them over to his desk. He stuck them in what appeared to be an electric pencil sharpener and after a few seconds pulled them out.

"Disabled," he said confidently.

"I hope you didn't ruin them. Otherwise my boss will have a fit," I said, crossing my arms.

"Nope, they're not ruined. All you have to do is reconnect them to whatever system you had them on. It's simple," he said, grinning. "Now, I have to say that I was impressed at how well you accomplished this mission. Good work!"

"Thanks," I replied, trying not to sound too excited, but I beamed inwardly. That was the smoothest mission I'd ever done. "The equipment worked well," I said.

"Good! I was pretty sure it would," Jason said, nodding. "Now let's look at these files. The notebook, please." I pulled the notebook out of my purse and handed it to him. He sat down at the desk and began looking at the pictures. At first, he looked pleased with what he saw, but then he looked confused.

"What's wrong?" I asked.

"I think we're missing a few pages," Jason replied worriedly.

"I made sure to take a picture of every page in the file, front and back," I said.

"Well, we're missing the most important ones. The ones with Mr. Brian's signature." Jason turned the notebook around toward me. "See?" he said, pointing to the pictures. "It goes from page nineteen to page twenty-two."

I sighed and face-palmed. "Are you kidding me?" I cried, frustrated with myself. "How did I not notice?"

"Simple mistake. It'll be all right. I'm guessing Brian hid those papers somewhere more secure," Jason said, obviously trying to be comforting. He wasn't helping. I was supposed to be an expert agent, and here I was making a simple mistake.

"So now we need to find out where he keeps those pages," Jason said. "While you're at work, try to find some info pointing toward where these pages are kept. If we can find them, then we've got all the info we need to kick Brian out and have a new guy take his place."

I nodded. *I can do this*, I told myself as I left Jason's office. *Just get your head in the game, girl!*

CHAPTER 5

I spent the next couple of weeks looking for the missing pages, but I couldn't find them. Mr. Zaiden was furious that I had brought him a file without the most important papers and that I was taking so long to find the missing ones.

"This is delaying my plans!" he told me. "I thought you were better than this." He slapped his desk and nearly spilled his coffee.

"Don't worry," I replied, trying to sound calm. "I'll find those papers. You keep on with your plans, and I'll take care of the papers."

"You'd better," he replied as I left the room.

After that distasteful meeting, I got a call from Jason, who was trying to help me brainstorm where the missing papers could possibly be hidden. So far we were no closer to finding the papers than when we'd started.

"We've been brainstorming for weeks, and we haven't found those papers," I said into my phone as I walked home. "We need a new plan."

"I'll keep thinking of ideas," Jason said with a sigh. "We'll find them somehow."

"We have to!" I replied, feeling a little anxious about Mr. Zaiden's response to my mistake.

Jason didn't reply for a moment. "I think I might have an idea," he said.

"Really? What is it?" I asked half-heartedly. I walked up the steps to my apartment door and unlocked it.

"I can't tell you now, but come by tomorrow morning, and I'll let you know what I've come up with," he replied. He sounded a little mysterious.

"If you say so," I said, stepping inside my room and closing the door. "See you then."

"Bye!" he replied and hung up.

Oh, this had better be a good plan, or I'm toast! I thought with a sigh.

A few hours later, I got a text from Sarah. "Want to meet for coffee?" she asked. I checked the time. I didn't have to be at the PBPC for another hour. *Might as well take a break and relax my mind*, I thought and sent her a yes.

Sarah had been meeting with me at the coffee shop a block away from my apartment once a week. Part of me was bugged that she wanted to get together so often—it took away time to do research for my jobs—but the other part of me began to enjoy our meetings. Sarah's sweet demeanor put me at ease and helped me relax from all the work stress.

Sarah stood outside the coffee shop, holding two paper cups. "Pumpkin latte for me. Mexican mocha for you," she said, placing the warm cup in my hand.

"Caught on, have you?" I replied, sitting at the table by the door.

Sarah sat across from me. "Isn't it a nice day?" she asked. There was a nice chill in the air, and fog had settled quietly over the city. One thing we definitely had in common was a love for cool weather.

I nodded and sipped my mocha. "So when are you returning to the academy to teach?"

She shrugged. "Probably January, but I'm not sure," she replied.

I glanced slyly at my sister. "Can I ask a personal question?"

She raised her eyebrows. "I suppose, since you're my sister and all," she said warily.

"Are you in Seattle because you're ... dating someone?" I asked suspiciously. So far I had yet to find out her reason for being around.

Sarah laughed and laughed. Finally, she choked out, "No! Where'd you get that idea?"

"Because it makes no sense why you're here away from your job," I replied seriously.

She managed to stop laughing and said, "I needed a change of pace. Seattle is much different than life at the academy as a teacher."

She quickly changed the subject, and I let her. I didn't buy into her excuses, but it didn't seem to matter that much. *Maybe we can be real sisters again*, I thought, and a smile crept onto my face.

r

The next morning I hurried to Jason's office, and he met me at the door. "Don't beat me here!" he said, grinning as he opened the door for me.

"What? You didn't think I'd be here this early?" I asked.

He shrugged. "Not really, but it's all right because I have a great plan."

We walked down the stairs to his desk, and he launched into his idea. "Okay, so is there a room in the PBPC office building you've never had access to?" he asked excitedly.

"Well, now that you mention it, yes. In the basement there's a computer room that's connected to the power plant. Only the people who are specially trained for the job can go down there. The equipment is very sensitive."

Jason said, "And if only a few people are allowed in—"

"—it's the perfect place to keep another safe with extremely important documents," I finished for him. "It's brilliant."

"Why, thank you," Jason replied with a bow.

"Uh, I meant that Mr. Brian's idea was brilliant," I said, raising an eyebrow at Jason. He frowned at me, so I quickly added, "But your idea was good, too."

"I'm glad you think so," Jason said with a wink. "Now let's start planning. How are you getting inside?"

We looked over the building plans and found an air duct that was big enough for me to crawl through and get inside the sensitive computer room.

"If I can use more of your equipment, then I think we can do this," I said after we finished mapping out a plan.

"Totally," Jason said with a nod. "Let's go for it!"

⌐

A few hours later, I sat at my desk at the PBPC, doing my usual routine: fixing what needed to be fixed, running programs, and doing security checks on the computer systems. After running the security checks, I pulled up the air-conditioning operating systems. Most of the building had been updated to the newest electronic system, which was smaller and circulated the air faster, but the basement hadn't been updated since Mr. Brian bought the building. Unfortunately, there happened to be a security system inside the duct, so if someone crawled through it, he or she would be detected.

"Okay Jason, what's your idea for getting through the security?" I asked quietly into my earring communication device as I looked over the diagram of the air duct.

"Clog the fan for the portion of the system next to the computer room," Jason instructed. "That will set the alarms off. I'm guessing Brian will ask you to turn the security off while someone tries to find out what's wrong. After they figure out the problem, sneak into the computer room, get what we're after, and get out. Then you can turn the security back on, and no one will know."

"Sounds simple," I replied as I stood up to leave my office. As I left, I grabbed my mini toolbox from beside the door. "Going to clog the fan now."

I made my way to the basement and found the fan. It had an easy-access hatch so it could easily be fixed if needed. I pulled my lockpick out of my purse and unlocked the hatch. I waited, listening for an alarm. "All clear," I whispered as I opened the door and looked inside.

"That means you won't need to turn off the security for someone to fix the problem," Jason said worriedly. "You need to find a way to jam the hatch. Otherwise you'll clog this fan for nothing."

"Got it," I replied, pulling a stuffed rat out of my bag.

Suddenly the sound of footsteps reached my ears. I turned to see a security guard walking toward me. "What are you doing?" she asked sternly.

"Systems check," I answered, stuffing the rat back into my

bag. "Some of the computer techs were complaining about the computer lab being too cold."

"Can't you fix that from the computer?" she asked, narrowing her eyes.

"With the new AC, yes, but not with this old machine," I said, glaring at her and putting my hands on my hips. "Unless I'm wrong. Are you an expert on air-conditioning?"

The guard rolled her eyes. "Whatever. Just hurry up and get out of here."

"Yes, ma'am," I said and turned back to my work. After I was sure she'd walked away, I pulled the "rat" back out of my purse.

"Inserting rat now," I said into my earpiece.

"Hurry up," Jason said. "You don't want that guard coming back."

"It's done," I said, quickly shutting the hatch. I grabbed a hammer from my toolbox and smashed the edge of the hatch into the wall. *That'll do*, I thought and ran back upstairs.

Just as I got back to my office and sat down in my chair, the alarm went off. "BASEMENT AIR DUCT MALFUNCTION" flashed on and off on my screen in bright red.

I pressed the intercom button on my computer and said, "Mr. Brian, we have a problem with the air duct in the basement."

A couple of minutes later, Mr. Brian walked into my office, and I showed him my screen. "I'll send Mark down there to get it fixed," he said after seeing the problem.

"All right," I said, and he left to get Mark.

"Wait for it," Jason said excitedly.

A few minutes later, my intercom beeped, and Mr. Brian spoke. "Amelia, please turn off the security system in the basement AC."

"I'm on it," I replied.

"Thanks," Mr. Brian said, and the intercom beeped off.

After a few clicks with my mouse, the security for the AC was off. "Done," I told Jason.

Fifteen minutes later, Mr. Brian walked past my office with Mark. "How did that rat get in? I thought we'd fixed the problem," I heard Mr. Brian say.

"I thought so too. I'll have to check it out. Also, we need to get that safety hatch fixed," Mark replied, and then I couldn't hear anything else they were saying.

"Looks like they've fixed the problem, and they forgot to tell me to turn the security back on," I told Jason as I stood up and left my office.

"Perfect. Head on down there and do your thing. I'm hacking into the basement security now," Jason said. I headed to the elevator and went down to the first floor, then took the stairs to the basement.

I walked back over to the air duct hatch. I looked around quickly to see whether any guards were around. After being sure no one was there, I pulled some pliers out of my toolbox and tugged at the edge of the hatch I'd smashed into the wall.

"Is that you making that racket?" Jason asked, sounding concerned.

"Uh, yeah. I smashed the hatch door so it couldn't open. Now I need it to open so I have a smooth getaway plan," I said as I pulled at the metal door. Finally, it pulled loose. "All right, I'm headed in," I said. I opened the door, put a stopper into the fan, and then crawled inside.

"I'm watching the security in the computer lab. So far so good. No one's inside," Jason informed me.

I continued crawling down the air duct. It was a tight squeeze but better than nothing. Finally, I reached the vent that entered the computer lab. "I'm here," I said. I pushed on the vent with my feet to see whether it would pop out.

"Don't kick the vent cover off," Jason warned. "The floor is concrete. That metal cover will clank loudly on the floor. Try to pull up."

"That will take longer," I said nervously, but I knew he was right. I pulled a utility knife from my toolbox and stuck it in the crack between the duct and the vent cover. I tried to pry it up, but the vent cover wouldn't budge.

"Okay, you need to hurry. Looks like some techs are headed your way," Jason urged.

"I'm trying! It's not working! I'll just have to kick it open," I said. "Can you find a way to distract everyone? Cause a commotion or something?"

"Let me see what I can do," Jason replied.

I waited, my heart pounding. After what seemed like forever, I heard the fire alarm sound.

"Okay, go now!" Jason said. I kicked the vent open and dropped into the room. I searched the room but couldn't find a safe.

"I don't see where Mr. Brian keeps these documents!" I cried, searching frantically through the drawers and cabinets.

"Look at the walls. Are there any cracks or uneven spots that could possibly be a hidden safe?" Jason suggested.

I ran my hand along the wall, feeling for any change in the surface.

"You'd better hurry!" Jason warned. "The fire drill isn't going to last that long."

I continued running my hand along the wall—nothing was there. "That didn't work. Maybe this theory was wrong," I said, pulling at my wig in frustration.

"You'd better go. A security guard is headed your way," Jason said.

I pulled a chair under the vent and then grabbed the vent cover. It had slid under the desk. As I grabbed it, I noticed that the floor under this part of the desk wasn't the same as the rest.

"Wait a minute. I think I've found it!" I cried excitedly. I felt along that portion of the floor and found an indent. I tugged at it, and the box slid up out of the ground. "Yes! This is it!" I told Jason. The safe needed a code to open it. I began typing in all the usual codes Mr. Brian used.

"Hurry up! The guard is swiping his card in the door!" Jason said. "You need to get out of there!"

"Not without those papers," I replied. I grabbed the chair and pushed it under the doorknob.

"That chair isn't going to keep the guard out for long," Jason warned.

I ran back to the safe and tried a few more codes. I could hear the guard banging on the door, trying to get in. "You've only got a few seconds before that door opens!" Jason yelled.

"One last code," I whispered to myself. I typed in Mr. Brian's first name. P-A-T-R-I-C-K. *There's no way he'd do something that easy*, I thought, and I stood up to leave. Suddenly the safe's door swung open.

"I'm in!" I told Jason.

"Get out of there now!" Jason's voice buzzed in my ear. "You can come back and get the papers another time. Right now you need to leave."

I sighed and slammed the safe shut. Jason was right; that chair wasn't going to hold the door much longer. I jumped up and grabbed the rim of the vent and pulled myself inside just as the guard opened the door to the computer lab. I didn't stay to see what the guard was doing. I hurried back down the air duct, opened the safety hatch, jumped out, and unclogged the fan. I slammed the hatch shut and ran up the stairs.

"You left the vent open," Jason said, his voice rather irritated.

"I didn't have a choice," I whispered as I hurried into the elevator. I reached my office a few minutes later and sat down.

Mr. Brian entered my office just after me. "Why didn't you turn the basement AC security back on?" he said angrily.

"You didn't tell me to," I replied.

"You should have done it anyways! Didn't you see us walk by earlier?" Mr. Brian asked, folding his arms.

"Yes, but I heard you say something about needing to fix something, so I left the security off," I explained, hoping he'd fall for my lie.

"Because of your failure to do your job, someone broke into the computer lab!" Mr. Brian yelled. "What were you thinking? Now we have a mess to deal with."

"I ... I'm sorry," I said, glancing down at my hands.

"Oh, you'd better be! If this happens again, you'll be fired!" Mr. Brian yelled and then exited the room.

"Oh boy," Jason's voice said. "That's ... lovely."

"Mm-hmm. Wonderful," I said sarcastically.

I finished my work and quickly left, feeling defeated. *Mr. Brian can't fire me! I can't let that happen*, I thought as I stomped down the street toward home. As I walked, it suddenly hit me how important it was for me to keep my job at the PBPC. *If I'm fired*, I thought worriedly, *then I can't help Jason prove that the PBPC has been shady, and I can't help Mr. Zaiden take over the company. I'll be in big trouble with all three employers. I will not be fired!*

As I walked through town, I saw the building connected to

Jason's office. I sighed and walked over to his office, unlocked the door, opened it, and descended the stairs.

Jason sat at his desk in the middle of his office, staring at a laptop. I stomped over to him and slammed the equipment I'd borrowed from him on the table. He looked up at me and raised his eyebrows. "What's up?" he asked. He tapped a few keys on the keyboard and closed his laptop.

"You can take your stupid stuff back," I said, gritting my teeth. I was ready to punch him in the face but restrained myself.

"Thanks. So are you okay?" he asked, his voice irritatingly calm.

"Am I okay? How thoughtful of you to ask," I said sarcastically, almost yelling at him. "I should have never agreed to help you. This is all your fault! Now I'm going to be fired by my boss because you just had to get involved. Everything was fine until you made your grand entrance into my life!" I slapped his desk and glared at him.

"Is your hand okay? You slapped the desk pretty hard," Jason said calmly, nodding at my hand.

"It's totally fine," I lied as I put my hands on my hips. My hand stung like crazy. "Do you have any genius plans to get me out of this mess you put me in? Huh?"

"Calm down. Everything will be fine," Jason said as he stood up. "We'll think up another plan, one less risky. You're right. It was totally my fault for sending you on such a risky plan. Next time we won't—"

"Oh, yeah. There'll totally be a next time, because the next time I'm caught, I'm fired! Didn't you hear Mr. Brian say that?" I yelled, stomping around to his side of the desk.

"I heard," Jason replied. "Let me think about it."

"Oh no. I'll think up a plan, since you're obviously not the expert you think yourself to be!" I turned around to leave, but he grasped my shoulder.

"Amelia, please, listen," he said, his voice still completely calm. I turned around to face him, folding my arms. "Look, I'm sorry, and you're right that I'm not perfect. But you're not perfect either. You can't do this alone."

"Oh yeah? Well, just watch me!" I cried and stomped out of the building.

I hurried home since it was getting dark. *What am I going to do? This is so stressful!* I thought as I walked up the stairs to my apartment. I pulled off my blonde wig, then pulled my apartment key from my pocket. As I stuck the key in the door, I realized the door was already unlocked.

One thing I do know. I didn't leave my door unlocked, I thought worriedly as I pushed the door open. The lights were off, but I could still see that my apartment was not how I'd left it. Papers were strewn across the floor, along with all the pillows and cushions from the couch and several other random things. I stepped inside and closed the door as quietly as possible. I tiptoed forward and peeked around the corner.

There was a person, dressed completely in black.

I turned back into the hallway and opened the drawer to the cabinet next to me. *Where's my Taser?* I wondered, setting my wig down and searching through the drawer as quietly as possible. It wasn't there. *Okay, let's get ready to use those self-defense skills*, I thought, hoping the intruder was unarmed.

I took a deep breath and rounded the corner. The intruder stood by my desk, back turned toward me. I wasn't going to let whoever it was go through my stuff. I crept closer. The intruder had something in his or her hand, but it didn't look like a weapon. It looked like a shirt.

Three, two, one, go, I told myself and then jumped on the unsuspecting intruder.

The intruder, who I could now tell was a girl, fell to the ground. She quickly shoved me off her, stood up, and darted for the door. I got up and ran after her, grabbing her arm to stop her. She twisted her arm, forcing me to let go. She tried to run again, but I tripped her with my foot. She sprawled on the floor, and I quickly jumped on top of her, pinning her to the ground.

"All right, what are you doing in my apartment?" I asked. I flipped on the light switch next to me so I could see.

The intruder was wearing a mask, but her long brown hair and bright-blue eyes were unmistakable. "Sarah?" I cried. I pulled the mask off her face, and my suspicions were confirmed. I couldn't speak for a moment, and rage boiled inside me. "What are you doing breaking into my apartment?"

"I didn't exactly break in," she replied, her voice sounding a little uncomfortable, probably because I was sitting on her. "I told the manager that I'd locked myself out of my apartment and needed help getting back in. He has a master key and got me inside."

"You pretended to be me?" I cried, horrified that my perfect, kind, Christian sister would do such a thing.

"Yeah. Now, could you get off? I can't breathe," she replied.

Slowly I got off and backed over to the front door so she couldn't leave. "How could you do this to me?" I asked, biting my lip.

Sarah stood up and shrugged. "Look, I can explain," she began, shoving her hand in her pocket.

"What's in your pocket?" I asked, putting my hand out. "Give it to me."

Sarah sighed, pulled a small camera out of her pocket, and handed it to me. It was full of pictures of all my files.

"This is why you've been trying to be buddies? So you can get pictures of all my files? So you can spy on me?" I cried.

"Rebecca, that's not it," Sarah said, shaking her head.

"Who hired you?" I asked.

"I can't tell you," Sarah replied, looking frustrated and upset.

"After all this nice 'Oh, let's get together and be sisters again,' you break into my house! You're just like everybody else. I can't trust anyone. Just leave!" I screamed. I opened the door, watched Sarah leave, and then slammed it shut. I locked the door and slid to the floor, crying.

How could she do this to me? I shouted in my head. After a few minutes, I wiped the tears from my eyes, got up, and headed for bed, not bothering to pick up anything. I tripped on something on the floor.

"What is that?" I muttered, picking it up. It was my red wig. *Sarah was holding this when I came in*, I realized, and then I walked back to the cabinet in the hallway where I'd set my blonde wig. *She saw both wigs*, I thought, fear rising in me. *Oh, Sarah, how could you?*

CHAPTER 6

The next morning I got a call from Mr. Zaiden, asking me to meet him that afternoon. As soon as I hung up, I got a call from Mr. Brian, telling me I'd better not be late for work and that there was a ton of paperwork I needed to do. As I was eating breakfast, Jason called and said he was going to be busy all day and that I didn't need to worry about helping him with anything.

Good thing, I thought as I hung up. *I don't need any more busyness added to my day!*

My work at the PBPC was quite stressful. Mr. Brian hadn't been kidding when he said he had a ton of paperwork for me to do. It was six o'clock in the evening by the time I was finished.

I went home and collapsed on the couch, not wanting to meet with Mr. Zaiden. Of course, my phone rang. "Hello?" I answered.

"Where are you? It's six thirty. I asked you to meet me this afternoon. Where are you?" Mr. Zaiden repeated impatiently.

"Uh, well, I had a ton of paperwork to do for Mr. Brian. He's kinda mad at me right now," I said, avoiding answering the question about my location.

"Well, get over here ASAP. I have an important assignment for you," Mr. Zaiden said, but before I could reply, he hung up.

"Not another assignment, especially not after the last one Jason gave me," I moaned. I got up slowly, switched my disguise to "Mariah," and headed out the door.

I reached Mr. Zaiden's office building and hurried inside. Just as I started up the final flight of stairs, I got a text message from Mr. Zaiden. "Busy. Please work on paperwork in your office and wait for me to come get you," it read. I wanted to continue up the stairs and find out what had made him suddenly too busy for our meeting, but I knew I was way behind on paperwork, so I went back down a flight of stairs to my office.

I sat at my desk and began filling out paperwork. Ten minutes later I had all the physical copies done, and I began working on the electronic copies. As I sent the last page to Mr. Zaiden, a file popped up on my computer. *What's this?* I wondered.

I clicked on the "open" button and waited. The file opened to show additional subfiles, each with a different label. There was a "PBPC" file, an "Assignments" file, a "$$$" file, an "Assassin" file, an "America" file, and a few files labeled with only numbers. The last file was labeled "MAX500."

What is all this? I thought. I'd never seen any of these files before. I clicked on the "PBPC" file. It required a password. I then clicked on all the files, and each required a password as well. *Why hasn't Mr. Zaiden showed me these files before?* I wondered. *Could this be his big plan that's so secretive?*

I decided to try the "PBPC" file again. I tried several codes, but they were all wrong. "5 ATTEMPTS LEFT" flashed across the screen. *Great*, I thought. *If I don't get this in five tries, it's going to lock me out. What could that code be?*

I searched my computer for any files marked "password" or "codes," but all I could find was a document on how to write secure passwords and "how to learn video game coding for dummies." Neither proved to be helpful.

I went back to the file. The words "5 ATTEMPTS LEFT" were still flashing across the screen. I tried the password for the front gate. "INCORRECT. 5 ATTEMPTS LEFT" flashed across the screen.

Five attempts left? I just used one … Shouldn't it say four *attempts left?* I wondered. *Maybe it's trying to tell me something.* I typed, "5ATTEMPTSLEFT" in as the password. A sign popped up that said no caps were allowed, so I redid it in lowercase letters.

"ACCESS GRANTED" flashed across the screen. *Wow! I'm surprised he picked something so easy*, I thought excitedly.

The file loaded quickly. Inside were the blueprints of the PBPC office building and a map of the other PBPC locations across the West Coast. Next to the blueprints were a bunch of notes I assumed Mr. Zaiden had written. Each note had a date next to it. The most recent one read, "Last attempt at the PBPC failed. My agent couldn't get me the documents I needed. Five attempts left."

The next one was from the day before. "Going to try another attempt at the PBPC. If all goes according to plan, then my master plan will be in effect."

All the rest of the notes had to do with the layout of the PBPC, notes from news articles regarding the company, and a lot of other uninteresting information I had gathered for Mr. Zaiden.

What is this master plan thing Mr. Zaiden referred to? I wondered, going back to the list of files. *None of these files are* labeled *"master plan"* ... *Maybe they all lead to his master plan.* Mr. Zaiden was becoming more and more mysterious the more I learned about him.

"Mariah."

I jumped and turned to face Mr. Zaiden.

"Oh, hello, sir. You startled me," I said with a forced laugh.

"I noticed," he replied with a nod. "Now come with me to my office."

"Yes, sir," I said, quickly exiting the page on my computer. *I hope he didn't see that,* I worried as I followed him upstairs.

As we entered his office, Mr. Zaiden said, "So, Mariah, I know we've been working on trying to put the PBPC down, but I think we need to let that rest for a moment."

"Probably," I agreed, thinking back to the problems from the day before.

"So I have a different job offer for you, and it's well paying too," Mr. Zaiden said as he sat down in his desk chair. He pulled a file out of his desk drawer and set it on the desk.

I smiled, sitting down in the chair opposite his desk. "Always willing to make a few more bucks," I replied.

"Good," he said, pushing the file toward me. "Then I have an assassination job for you."

I felt my face growing pale. "Now wait a minute, sir," I cautioned. "I never agreed to be an assassin. You know that."

"But you'd do so well at it, and we need to stop this person because they know too much," he argued, leaning back in his chair. I opened my mouth to argue, but he continued. "You probably never realized it, but all the training I've been giving you since you started working for me has led up to this point. You have all the training you need to do the job. You just have to use it."

"Yeah, right," I muttered as I picked up the file off his desk. I opened it and gasped. The picture inside was of Jason.

"No," I replied flatly, tossing the file back onto his desk. I glared at Mr. Zaiden as coldly as possible. My heart was racing.

Mr. Zaiden sighed. "That's too bad, Mariah." He picked up the file and opened his desk drawer. "I guess I'll just have to dispose of you," he said, looking me in the eye.

Fear gripped me; I knew exactly what he meant. "You can't dispose of me!" I cried. "I'm your best agent!"

"And I trained you. I can always train someone else," Mr. Zaiden replied, sticking the file in the drawer and closing it. He opened another drawer and pulled out a gun, pointing it straight at my head. "So what will it be?" he said, an evil grin spreading across his face.

My heart was racing. This couldn't happen. "All right! Fine. I'll do it!" I cried, trying to stay calm and failing.

Mr. Zaiden smiled and pulled the gun away from my face. "Wise decision," he said. Keeping the gun trained on me, he pulled the file back out of the drawer and handed it to me. "I knew you wouldn't let me down," he said with a fierce glare.

But I'm letting Jason down, I thought as I stood up slowly, my legs wobbling from fear. Mr. Zaiden escorted me out of the building and to the front gate.

"Don't come back until the job is done. Do you understand?" Mr. Zaiden asked sternly.

"Yes, sir," I replied, my heart still pounding.

"All right then. Have a good evening," Mr. Zaiden said, smiling pleasantly. He patted me on the back, then pushed me through the gate. I backed away slowly, keeping my eye on his hand with the gun. After I knew I'd gone far enough so he couldn't shoot me, I took off for my apartment.

What have I gotten myself into? I thought angrily as I raced home. *I'm no murderer!*

I hardly slept that night. I lay awake, worrying about my new assignment.

I got up the next morning and got ready for the day slowly, not knowing exactly what to do. *I could run away,* I thought but then decided it wouldn't do me any good. Mr. Zaiden was a pro at tracking people down. I thought about warning Jason to move to another country and then telling Mr. Zaiden he'd moved, but then I realized Mr. Zaiden would probably just send me overseas to find Jason.

Is there a way out of this that doesn't involve someone being killed? I worried as I ate breakfast.

I was getting ready for work at the PBPC, putting my blonde wig on and doing my makeup, when I got a message on my laptop from Mr. Brian. I walked over to read it.

"Meeting with some investors today. Don't worry about coming in today. See you tomorrow. Patrick Brian."

I sent a quick thank-you reply and closed my laptop. I sighed and went back to look at myself in the mirror. I was pretty much finished with my "Amelia" disguise. *Do you ever get to just be you?* I wondered. Seeing myself as "Amelia" and "Mariah" all the time had become so normal; it was almost weird to be Rebecca.

I sighed and went into the living room to sit down on the couch. *I'll get out of this costume later,* I decided and began reading the newspaper. My thoughts didn't stay on the news, though. All I could think about were Mr. Zaiden and Jason. Mr. Zaiden had always seemed so dependable and supportive, always encouraging me to use my potential. I didn't want to lose his trust now.

But there was Jason. He was nothing like my other bosses. He was way younger, and he wasn't ever fazed by anything and never lost his cool. *But he hasn't been your boss for long, and his last idea got you in serious trouble*, my mind told me. *Do you really want to side with him?*

Before I could think of the answer, my phone dinged. I walked over to the kitchen table and picked it up. It was a text from Sarah. It read, "Would you be willing to meet me for lunch? I understand if you don't want to."

I quit reading and set my phone down. "No way, sister. Not after what you did to me," I muttered and went back to my newspaper.

That afternoon I went to make myself some lunch, then realized I needed to go to the store. The fridge was almost empty. "I need more days off if I don't have time to even go shopping," I said as I put my shoes on. I grabbed my purse, and after making sure my ID matched my "Amelia" costume, I left my apartment.

I glanced up at the sky full of clouds, wondering whether it would rain. Luckily there wasn't much traffic on the streets or in the air for the afternoon, so it made for a peaceful walk to the grocery store.

I picked up a few groceries and headed home. As I walked, it began to rain. *Perfect timing. Raining while I'm carrying groceries*, I thought sarcastically as I picked up the pace. As I walked up to the crosswalk, my phone rang.

"Are you kidding me?" I said, setting down one bag of

groceries so I could pull my phone out of my purse. Mr. Brian was calling. "Hello?" I answered, trying to hide my irritation.

"Just what do you think you were doing, spying on my meeting with our investors?" he cried angrily.

"What are you talking about?" I asked, completely confused.

"Don't play dumb. You know exactly what I'm talking about," he replied. I had no comeback since I had no idea what he was talking about. "What were you thinking?" he continued yelling. "I almost lost them as investors! Luckily my good people skills convinced them to continue supporting us."

"Good people skills. Right," I said, pulling my earpiece out of my purse. After sticking it in my ear, I put my phone back in my purse and picked up my grocery bag. The whole time Mr. Brian continued ranting and raving about how he'd almost lost his investors, and he continued bragging about his "good" people skills.

I crossed the street and kept listening to Mr. Brian talk without replying. "Are you still there?" he finally asked.

"Yup," I replied.

"Well, let this be a warning to you. Unless you have a good explanation for what happened—"

"But it didn't happen," I interrupted him. "I am walking home from the grocery store. I couldn't have been spying on you."

"Oh yeah. Likely story. And I completely doubt it. When you come in to work tomorrow, you'd better have a good story to tell, or else you're fired!" he cried.

"Don't make any rash decisions," I warned, but he hung up before I could say more. I sighed and continued walking down the street. *What a lovely day*, I thought sarcastically, looking down at my groceries to see whether they were still okay after sitting in the rain. I looked up just as I bumped into someone.

"Oh, I'm sorry. I wasn't paying attention," I apologized to the man.

"Obviously," the man said, his voice rather gruff. He looked homeless, his clothes ratty, his hair a mess, and his long beard rather dirty. And he stank.

"Well, I'm sorry. See you later," I said, trying to step around him.

He stepped into my way.

"Please get out of my way," I said firmly.

"Sure," he replied. He stood still for a second; then, quick as a flash, he grabbed one of my bags of groceries and took off down the street.

"Hey! Give that back!" I cried, taking off after him.

He darted down an alley, and I followed. I chased him through several alleys before I stopped to look around. This wasn't a good part of town. It was pouring rain now, and I was all alone.

I don't care about the groceries. I just need to get out of here, I told myself and began making my way out of the neighborhood.

I was almost back in my neighborhood when a car whipped around the corner and pulled to a stop right next to me. I kept walking, acting as natural as possible. The driver rolled down the nearest window.

"Whatcha doing in this part of Seattle?" he asked, leaning out of the window. I couldn't see the speaker in the pouring rain, but I recognized the voice instantly. Jason.

"Taking a walk," I replied casually, then turned to keep walking.

"Do you need a ride?" he called, almost sounding commanding.

"No, but thanks for the offer," I said without turning around. I didn't want him to find out where I lived.

I heard a car door open. "Let me rephrase that, Rebecca," Jason said.

I turned to face him. He was holding a gun.

"Who's Rebecca?" I tried to bluff, but Jason just laughed.

"Don't give me that. You're a good actress, but you aren't fooling me. Now, will you please hop in and let me give you a ride? It's only the gentlemanly thing for me to do," he said, smiling the whole time.

I considered making a run for it when the homeless man stepped out from the shadow of the house next to us. With a gun in one hand and my groceries in the other, he walked straight up to me. "Do as the man says. Here's your food back," the man said, holding out the bag to me.

I took the groceries angrily and rolled my eyes. "Okay, whatever. I'll come. Thank you for your generosity," I said, stomping over to Jason's car.

Jason walked around to the other side of the car, opened the passenger door, and motioned for me to get in. I climbed in and sat down. Jason closed my door and walked over to the driver's side.

Had the homeless man not been there, I would have gotten away easily, but at the moment, I couldn't think of a way out. *How could Jason know my real name?* I wondered, leaning back in the passenger's seat, feeling shocked and defeated. *I didn't tell him who I really was. How did he figure it out? Why is everything going wrong today?*

"Hey, dude, thanks for helping me," Jason said to the homeless man.

"No problem. I'm always ready to help ya," he replied.

"Good! Well, see you later," Jason said with a cheerful wave. He got in, closed his door, and started the car.

"What's all this for?" I asked, turning to face Jason. I was ready to explode.

"I'm not taking questions until we get to my office," he said, turning the car around and driving down the street.

I sat back in my seat, trying to gain my composure and think through my options. I decided against jumping from a moving car without protection. I realized I'd have to think of an escape plan once we got to Jason's office.

I knew I shouldn't have trusted him. He was too ... too nice, I thought angrily. *How could I have been so dumb?*

I sat looking out the window, ignoring Jason the whole ride to his office. Jason pulled into a parking spot behind the building and turned off the car. He turned to me and smiled.

"Here we are," he said. "You can leave your groceries in the car for now. It's cold enough outside—they won't go bad." Then he stepped out of the car and motioned for me to get out.

This is your chance! I thought as I got out of the car. *He put his gun away. I'd better take the chance.*

Jason walked over to the door and began punching in the pass code, his back turned toward me.

I turned around and dashed down the street. Five steps later, I fell flat on the ground. "What happened?" I muttered. I felt like I'd run into a brick wall.

Jason walked over to me and helped me up. "You shouldn't try any tricks," he said, his voice calm and patient as though he were speaking to a kid.

"Don't baby me," I replied, pushing him away. I promptly lost my balance and began to fall, but Jason quickly caught me.

"Careful," he said, grinning at me.

"What did you do to me?" I asked, frustrated that Jason was now helping me down the stairs.

"I shot you with my new Taser gun. My buddy Matt and I have been working on it for a long time. Basically, instead of giving you an electric shock, it just turns you into a jellyfish for about ten minutes without the aftereffects of a normal Taser," he answered excitedly. "Pretty cool, huh? That's why I nicknamed my gun Jellyfish."

"Do you know how it feels?" I asked, gritting my teeth. If I hadn't been turned into a jellyfish right then, I would have punched him.

"Totally. Somebody had to be the test dummy, and I picked the wrong side of the coin," Jason said. He sat me down in his office chair and began rummaging through his desk.

"Are you searching for the antidote?" I asked sarcastically. *If he finds it, I'll tackle him*, I thought.

"No, I'm looking for ... aha!" he exclaimed, pulling a box of doughnuts from the bottom drawer. "I'm sure you have a lot of questions for me, so I have to be prepared." He grabbed a powdered doughnut from the box and took a large bite. "Okay, now I'm good to go," he said, his mouth still full of food.

"I plead the fifth," I replied. *At least I'll be relaxed during this interrogation*, I thought with a sigh.

Jason didn't say anything. He just kept eating his doughnut and watching me expectantly. His calm manner infuriated me. In the middle of the awkward silence, we heard a bunch of banging. "What is that?" I asked. It almost sounded as though it were below us instead of above us.

That's impossible, I told myself. *We're in the basement.*

Jason didn't seem to hear me. He listened intently to the banging. I began to listen too. At first it just sounded like someone was making a huge ruckus, but then I realized the banging was actually Morse code. I missed most of the message, but I could make out that whoever was sending this message wanted to know whether Jason had brought something or, I assumed, someone.

"Is that your boss?" I asked, raising my eyebrows.

"Is what my boss?" Jason asked. His face looked completely blank, except for his eyes. He was quite obviously lying.

"The person who just sent you a Morse code message," I replied, rolling my eyes.

"No, it's just a friend," Jason answered, reaching for another doughnut. "Now, what questions do you have for me?"

"Why did you call me Rebecca?" I asked, trying to state the question indifferently.

"Because it's your name," Jason answered. He motioned with his hands for me to keep going.

"Okay, why do you think that's my name?" I asked, tilting my head. I hoped my confidence would make him worry he was wrong.

"I heard it from a friend," he answered, shrugging.

"What friend do you have who would know me?" I asked, trying to act like I was just playing along. Meanwhile I ran through a list of people from whom he could have possibly found out my identity. *Could it be the apartment manager? My next-door neighbor?* I wondered.

"Would you like to meet my friend? It may help us get to the point quicker," Jason said, crossing his arms.

The look on Jason's face made it obvious he wanted me to meet his friend, so I decided it'd be best to put it off. "No thanks."

Jason paced around, deep in thought, for a few minutes. I was beginning to feel like myself again, and I began planning how to get away when Jason walked back over to me.

"You know what? I think this just isn't fair," he said, shaking his head apologetically.

"You're right. It's so not fair for you to kidnap me and interrogate me when I work for you," I said angrily.

"That's not what I'm talking about," he said, raising an eyebrow at me. "I'm talking about me making you admit that your name is Rebecca. Rebecca Sanders, that is."

I opened my mouth to speak, then closed it again. I didn't want to say anything to help him achieve his goal. And I couldn't believe he also knew my last name.

"I think we should make a deal," Jason continued, and he began to pace back and forth in front of me. "I'll tell you a secret if you tell me what I want to know."

"I'm not a toddler. I don't want to hear your secrets," I replied, folding my arms. The jellyfish feeling was gone now.

"Well, I guess I'll just tell you then," Jason said. He paused for a minute, looking thoughtful. Finally, he said, "My name isn't Jason."

"What?" I said, raising an eyebrow. "You aren't Jason? Then ... wait, are you not the Jason who worked for PBPC?"

"Oh, I am the Jason who worked for PBPC. It's just that that isn't my real name. Just like you go by Amelia when you're working at the PBPC and by Mariah when you're working with the Zaiden boss," Jason (or whatever his name was) said, putting his hands on his hips. "Aren't I right?"

"How can you be sure that Mariah isn't my name or that Amelia isn't my name?" I asked. I was running out of lies to tell.

"I searched for you on the Internet by both names. You came up as Amelia working for PBPC, but no Mariah came up. And I searched for birth records of both of those names. The only names I could find identical to your cover-ups were too old or young to be you," Jason said, nodding triumphantly as he finished.

"Too old or too young?" I asked, hanging onto my last hope that I could fake being older or younger than eighteen.

"Too old as in you'd have to be forty-nine and too young as in you'd have to be seven," Jason answered.

"Oh," I said, not sure what to say to that. I couldn't believe that he'd done so much research on me, and I hadn't done any research on him. I decided to change the subject. "So what's your real name?"

"My real name is Luke Mason," he replied.

"Luke Mason?" I repeated. I knew that name from when I was a kid. I stopped to think for a moment. Why did I know that name? Then I remembered. Before I moved, when I was still going to Truth Academy, I knew one kid at school whose name was Luke Mason. *No wonder he looked familiar*, I thought, still feeling shocked.

"I know. It's rather surprising," Jason, or rather Luke, said.

"Uh, yeah," I said. For some strange reason, I felt almost excited to be meeting a friend from my childhood, but at the same time I was angry that he would betray me.

"Imagine my surprise when I found out who you were—my playmate from kindergarten," Luke said.

"So ... how'd you know I was me?" I asked mostly to myself before realizing I had spoken aloud. "I mean, why are you guessing who you think I am?" I tried to recover, but it was no use.

"Don't try to keep faking it. Anyways, I had my suspicions when I first met you and you got me fired," Luke explained, "but it wasn't until my friend confirmed my suspicions that I knew you were Rebecca."

"Okay, seriously, who is this friend of yours? I seriously

doubt you and I share any friends," I said doubtfully. *I don't have friends anyways,* I thought, annoyed.

"You can meet my friend yourself," Luke said, grinning at me with pure excitement. "Are you feeling better now, or do you still feel like Jell-O?" he asked.

"I'm fine. Thanks for asking," I said, standing up. I still felt a little wobbly, but I wasn't going to tell him that.

"Good. Then help me move this desk," he said.

He started pushing the desk in my direction, so I walked over by him and began helping him push the desk. It slowly scraped across the floor, eventually revealing a small trapdoor.

"Thanks for helping. It's hard to move this bad boy all by yourself," Luke said, patting his desk.

"You keep a trapdoor under your desk," I said, raising an eyebrow at him.

"Of course, I mean, who doesn't?" he asked, grinning at me.

"I would have put it somewhere more accessible. Otherwise you have to move the desk and make such a loud racket every time you want to go through the trapdoor!" I said, putting my hands on my hips.

"But if it was more accessible, it would be easier to find," Luke countered. He pointed at me and nodded. "Never would have thought of it, would you?"

I shrugged. I probably wouldn't have, but I also remembered the time I'd showed up early, and he was shoving his desk back into place. *He must have been meeting with his friend just before I showed up,* I thought suspiciously. *I wondered why he asked why I was already back.*

Luke opened the hatch and waved toward it. "Ladies first," he said, grinning at me.

"Why, thank you. You're such a gentleman," I replied sarcastically, then climbed down the ladder.

Reaching the floor, I turned to look around. This room was much larger than his tiny office above us. There was a row of shelving along the left wall, and on the right was a long desk with several laptops. Along the back wall were a bunch of boxes and a door to another room. In the center of the room was a round table with a black box on top, which looked like one of the latest high-tech computers I'd seen on TV. Those things were very cool and super expensive. Even Mr. Zaiden didn't have one.

Luke finished climbing down the ladder and closing the hatch, and now he stood beside me. "Pretty cool, huh? And even though you can't tell right now, our lights can change colors and do a little disco-like thing. This place is sooo awesome!" he exclaimed, bouncing up and down. He acted as if this were the first time he'd ever been down here.

"You sure have a lot of high-tech stuff down here," I said, walking around the room. I was in awe of the equipment. I pointed at the table in the middle of the room. "Is that what I think it is?"

"That depends on what you think it is," Luke replied, wriggling his eyebrows. "If you think it's a giant doughnut, you're wrong, sadly. But if you think it's the latest computer projection system, fully equipped with all the cool gadgets, then you are correct. Let me show you how it works," he said excitedly. He turned it on and pointed out all the features. "You see, once you have it set up with another computer or laptop device—this is set up to our mainframe computer—it works just like any other computer, only as a projector. It has a sensor, so you just use your hand to select things, make things bigger or whatever, and the sensor knows what you want.

You just have to learn the right-hand signals. Plus it has voice command for Internet searches so you don't have to type anything. Isn't this so cool?" he asked, clapping his hands.

"I have to admit this is the coolest thing I've ever seen in person," I answered, nodding. I really wanted to try it out, but I didn't want to distract myself from the problem at hand. Jason, who was actually Luke, had betrayed me. I couldn't trust him anymore, and I needed to be thinking of finding a way out of here.

"Oh, I forgot! I'm supposed to introduce you to my friend. Here, have a doughnut while I go get her," Luke said, grabbing a box of doughnuts off the shelf. He placed it in my hands and left the room through the back door.

Now's your chance! I told myself, setting the box of doughnuts on the desk full of laptops. *Just leave through the hatch.* I ran over and climbed up the ladder and opened the hatch as quietly as possible. Just as I'd opened it enough for me to get out, the lights turned red, and a mechanical voice started saying, "Alert! Alert! Hatch has been opened by unauthorized personnel." It kept repeating this message over and over. Before I could fully get out of the hatch, Luke was back in the room. He pulled me out of his office and back into the lower basement.

"You didn't tell me there was an alarm," I said, crossing my arms. Luke ran over to one of the laptops, clicked a few buttons, and then the alarm quit blaring.

"Sorry about that," Luke said, turning to face me. "I didn't expect you to try to make a run for it." He sounded so casual and trusting. *How can he act that way after betraying me? Acting all trust-like?* I thought angrily. I glared at him and shook my head, not having anything to say.

"Well, let me introduce you to my friend," Luke said,

pointing to the door on the back wall. Just then out walked Sarah.

"What?" I cried.

"Rebecca, meet Sarah. Sarah, meet Rebecca," Luke said cheerfully.

"Nice to meet you," I said, rolling my eyes. *So Jason—I mean, Luke—hired Sarah to break into my apartment*, I thought angrily.

"I have to admit. You're pretty amazing at disguises," Sarah said, walking up to me. "If I wasn't related to you, I wouldn't have recognized you as the same girl." She tugged at the blonde wig on my head. I hadn't secured it as well today since I hadn't ended up going to work, so the wig came off easily.

"Okay, I totally see the resemblance now," Luke said, nodding. "You're definitely identical twins, except Rebecca has blonde eyebrows." He now looked puzzled.

"Okay, I admit it. I wear wigs, and I dye my eyebrows. Is that all you wanted me to say?" I asked angrily.

"Or how about 'My name is Rebecca, and I'm your sister' for a start?" Sarah said, tilting her head.

"You've been disowned," I muttered, glaring at her. Sarah looked hurt.

I sighed. If Sarah was helping Luke, there was no way I could keep up this charade. "So you're just going to throw me in jail, huh?" I asked, avoiding telling them about myself.

"No, we're waiting for you to admit the truth," Luke said.

"Then I go to jail. I see. Well, then you'll be old and gray before you make me admit to anything," I replied.

"Actually, we could put you in jail for many other reasons before we put you in jail for faking your IDs and such," Sarah said.

"Look, you have a lot of info that can help us," Luke said.

"We have some info that can help you. We need to work together so we can stop Mr. Brian from stealing money from people. But, more importantly, we need to stop Mr. Zaiden from completing his master plan."

"How do you know about that?" I asked, curious.

"Learned it all from you," he replied.

I was shocked, but Sarah quickly explained, "That first day we met for lunch, I gave you a hug, remember? I placed a tracking and listening device on the back of your neck to monitor your conversations and where you were going. From that device we learned Mr. Zaiden's location and then confirmed that you worked for him."

"And when you were on your computer that day and found those secret files from Mr. Zaiden, did you wonder how they got there?" Luke asked. I nodded. "That was us. We found those files by accident one day while trying to hack some of Mr. Zaiden's files. We couldn't break the codes, so we decided to pop it up on your computer and let you do the work for us."

"How'd you know I'd be at my computer then?" I asked.

"Uh, well, we uh ..." Sarah tried to answer but looked rather embarrassed.

"That text you got saying Mr. Zaiden was in a meeting? That was me. We also texted Mr. Zaiden saying you were working on important paperwork that needed to be done and that you'd be busy for a few minutes. You both totally fell for it," Luke said, grinning. He was obviously trying hard not to laugh.

"So what is this master plan of his?" I asked.

"We're not entirely sure, but we've noticed he's been trying to take over other power companies across America, not just on the West Coast," Sarah said.

"He's also been searching the Internet for info about

military weapons, nukes, and other powerfully destructive things," Luke added.

"And that information I got for him was top-secret government stuff," I said, putting a finger on my chin thoughtfully. "You don't think he could possibly be trying to do something government related."

"That's what we need to find out," Luke said.

"And that's why we need you. If this is as dangerous as we think it is, we need someone on the inside helping us learn as much as possible. Otherwise we won't be able to stop him," Sarah said seriously.

"Why doesn't the government take care of this problem?" I asked.

"They don't view Mr. Zaiden as a big threat right now. But they'll change their minds when ... when ... uh, I don't know, something really bad happens!" Luke replied, his eyes wide with excitement.

"And why are you two trying to stop Mr. Zaiden if the government isn't even doing anything?" I asked. "Who hired you?"

"I told you, we're kind of self-employed," Luke said.

"Right. Just kind of," I said, rolling my eyes.

"Rebecca, we need you to help us," Sarah finished. "You're perfect for the job, and we can't accomplish our goal without you."

"But we also need to know we can trust you," Luke said.

"I need to know *I* can trust *you*," I replied, "because at the moment I don't."

"Look, this is a big gamble for all of us. Are you in?" Luke asked.

I said, "But Mr. Zaiden—"

"Mr. Zaiden may have seemed like someone who cared

about you a lot, but he's an actor," Sarah interrupted me. "You yourself should know how easy it is to pretend you care about someone. He's an assassin. He is only going to keep you working for him as long as you're useful, and then he'll get rid of you permanently—he'll kill you. That's not the kind of man you should trust."

"I know I don't seem super trustworthy right now, having pretended to be someone I'm not, but it was the only way for this plan to work," Luke said. "And now I've been in your shoes."

"What do you mean?" I asked, still upset at them.

"Well, I know what it's like pretending to be someone else and trying to keep someone working for you when there are so many reasons not to trust one another," Luke explained.

I nodded. That was true. It was hard to keep people's trust when you were constantly pretending to be someone you weren't.

"And right now you have two options. You work for us and get a better record with the police, or you go straight to jail. Your choice," Sarah said softly.

"That's not much of a choice," I said, shaking my head reluctantly. "I guess I'll help you ... if you tell me who you're working for."

"It's a deal," Luke replied quickly. "But like I said before, we're sort of self-employed with connections to the government. The deal is, we're trying to prove to the government that these guys really are a threat. So now you're helping us?" He raised his eyebrows expectantly.

The answer wasn't as clear as I was hoping for, but it would have to do. "I guess so."

"Thank you!" Sarah said, hugging me. Then she whispered

in my ear, "And I'm sorry for breaking into your house. Will you forgive me?"

I shrugged. "I don't know," I replied, although I thought, *Probably not.*

After eating some doughnuts Luke insisted we eat, I got ready to go home.

"I'll drive you home," Luke offered.

I began to decline, but then I realized Luke and Sarah already knew where I lived, so I didn't have to keep that a secret from them anymore. "Okay," I agreed, feeling slightly relieved that I didn't have to walk home. Luke and I climbed up the ladder and then up the stairs and out of the building. Sarah stayed in the computer room, as it was called, to continue doing research on the PBPC and Mr. Zaiden.

As I got in the car, it suddenly hit me. I still couldn't go back to work with Mr. Zaiden until Jason, actually Luke, was dead. "Luke, we have a problem," I said as he started the car.

"What's that?" he asked.

"I can't go back to work until I've assassinated Jason Lenard," I said, slouching back in my seat.

"Are you serious?" he asked, his face completely shocked.

"Yes," I replied. "Mr. Zaiden gave me the assignment yesterday. I can't go back to work until you're dead. That was his order."

"Well, that's a problem. Were you actually planning on assassinating me?" he asked, totally calm.

"Well, no ... I mean, well ... I don't know. I didn't know what to do," I answered, feeling rather ashamed that I'd ever considered doing something so outrageous.

"Well, we'll think of a way to fix the problem. Maybe I can wear wigs and dye my eyebrows until the mission is over or something," Luke said, winking at me.

I rolled my eyes. He was taking this situation way too lightheartedly.

Luke pulled the car into the parking lot of my apartment, parked the car, and turned to face me. "Don't worry. We're a team now, and we'll figure out how to do this."

"I hope so," I said, sighing.

I got out of the car and grabbed my groceries. I turned to enter the building, when Luke said, "Rebecca, I need to ask you something."

I turned back to face him. "Yes?" I asked.

"Well, remember we used to go to the same school when we were younger," he began, speaking slowly and seriously, "and you always seemed to be a strong Christian, but then after your dad left, you sort of changed. You weren't the same person anymore, and soon you left too. So I guess my question is, are you still a Christian?" He fixed his eyes intently on me as he waited for the answer.

I shrugged, not really wanting to answer. "Does it matter?" I asked. I knew I wasn't a Christian, and I didn't really want to be one. And I definitely didn't want to be preached at.

"I believe it does matter. I also believe that with God all things are possible, and I want you to know that I believe that with His help we can do this," Luke said, smiling softly. "That's why you don't need to be worried. I was just hoping you'd have the same assurance, but I'm afraid you don't." His voice was full of sympathy.

"I don't need to be preached at. It's not like I don't know this stuff," I said, shrugging. "But thanks anyway." I spun on my heel and left.

CHAPTER 7

The next day I went to the PBPC to work. I decided to continue working there until we thought of a convincing way to fake Jason's, or Luke's, death.

I sat in my office, going through the usual routine. I didn't feel the excitement of being a double agent. I felt like everyone could see right through me. I suddenly felt more like Rebecca than Amelia.

I typed vigorously on my laptop, doing system reviews and paperwork. *Don't let that bother you,* I told myself, putting on the best face of confidence I could. *Luke has Sarah on his side. If he didn't, he'd never have guessed who you were. Just stay calm.*

I scanned the security camera feed and noticed that one of the camera's lenses was out of focus. I was heading down the hall toward the security room so I could fix the problem when I bumped into Mr. Brian as he barreled down the hall.

"Watch it!" he said, glaring at me.

"Sorry 'bout that," I said and continued on.

"Wait, just a minute. Where are you going?" Mr. Brian said.

"To the security room," I answered without turning around.

"And what for?" Mr. Brian asked, coming up next to me and matching my pace. He looked very upset.

"To fix the outdoor camera D. The focus is off," I explained, opening the security door.

Mr. Brian followed me into the room. "Don't you have something else you need to be doing?" he asked, glaring at me.

I raised an eyebrow at him. "I don't know," I said, and then I remembered. I was supposed to meet with him this morning and explain my supposed spying on him from the day before.

"You're supposed to be in my office right now. So move it!" Mr. Brian said.

"All right! I'm going! But you'd better have Andy fix the camera. It's totally fuzzy," I said, exiting the room.

"Okay, I'll let Andy know," Mr. Brian said, rolling his eyes. He pulled his radio off his belt and called Andy, telling him to fix the camera.

We went up the elevator and entered Mr. Brian's office. He took his seat behind the desk. "Are you ready to explain yourself?" he asked, crossing his arms.

"Uh, yeah," I said, sitting down in the other chair. I took a deep breath and thought fast. "Well, first off, I wasn't spying on you," I said, tilting my head.

"Then what were you doing, peeking into the meeting room window?" Mr. Brian asked impatiently.

"Because I left, um ..." I paused, trying to think of a good excuse, even though I knew nothing of the situation. "I left a pair of socks on the windowsill," I said, acting embarrassed.

"You what?" Mr. Brian exclaimed, looking surprised. "You left a pair of socks on the windowsill? What in the world would you do that for?"

"Well, there's actually a logical explanation. You see, I have a pair of socks I use for fixing equipment that's greasy or oily. I wear an old pair of socks on my hands so I don't get my hands greasy and then get other things greasy when I touch them," I explained. The explanation was at least the truth, unlike my story.

"Why don't you wear gloves?" Mr. Brian asked, looking half convinced.

I shrugged. "It's just one of those quirky things I do. I don't like getting my work gloves greasy," I said.

Mr. Brian sighed. "I guess that's that then," he said, leaning back in his chair. "I was worried there for a minute that I'd have to fire one of my best employees."

"Oh, well, I'm sorry I worried you. I should have waited until your meeting was over to get those socks, but I was embarrassed that they were on the windowsill during your meeting," I said, acting sheepish.

"It probably wouldn't have mattered. I didn't notice them," Mr. Brian said, waving a hand at me. "Now you get back to work."

"Yes, sir," I replied and left his office. *Well, that was easier than I thought*, I said to myself as I headed back to my office.

***

That evening I went to Luke's office, this time looking like my normal self. I unlocked the door and hurried down the stairs, but the office was empty. *They must be in the computer room*, I thought, but the desk was still in place. I pulled out the watch I'd gotten from Luke and sent him a quick message, asking his whereabouts.

A few seconds later he replied, "In computer room. Come on down." I looked up from my watch at the heavy metal desk. I sighed and started pushing on it. After five minutes of loud scraping, I could finally open the hatch. I hurried down the ladder, which set off the alarm.

"Hey, Rebecca!" Sarah yelled over the loud siren. Luke scrambled over to his laptop and shut off the alarm.

"Sorry about that. We need to get your fingerprints entered into the security system," Luke said, hurrying over to the hatch and closing it.

"So what's the plan for faking your death?" I asked, getting straight to the point.

"How do you think Mr. Zaiden would want you to prove my death?" Luke asked, putting a finger to his lips thoughtfully.

"I don't know. He told me he's been training me to do this kind of thing ever since I began working for him, but I never would have guessed it," I replied, shrugging.

"Is there some other way that he asks you to prove other assignments?" Sarah asked.

"Most of the time my assignments involve bringing something back to him that he asks for," I replied.

"Some evidence," Luke said, nodding.

"But what kind of evidence would prove that you killed someone?" Sarah asked, grimacing at her own words.

"Blood and a fingerprint," I replied, snapping my finger. "That's all I need! We'll just put Luke's fingerprint on a piece of paper and smear some blood on something, and we're good," I said, nodding. "This might work."

"Problem, The fingerprint is perfect, but a little blood from pricking myself with a needle won't cut it," Luke said, shaking his head.

"We'd need more like a rag soaked in blood," I said. "Like, if I was cleaning up after the mess."

Sarah shivered. "This is grossing me out. I'm going to go do some research. You guys can figure this out on your own," she said and hurried into the other room.

"You could go to a blood bank and have some blood drawn and bring it back," I suggested.

"The blood bank wouldn't give the blood to us. They'd save it for someone who needed it," Luke said.

"Do you happen to have any doctor friends who'd be willing to do that for you?" I asked hopefully. He did seem to have a friend for every job.

"Uh, yeah, but he's in Hawaii right now," Luke replied.

"That won't work," I said, shaking my head.

"I could do it myself," Luke said, but I quickly vetoed that idea.

"That might be dangerous," I said.

"Sarah could do it. She's got first-aid training," Luke suggested.

"She just left because she couldn't stand us talking about blood. I think the best bet is going to the blood bank and stealing the blood," I said.

"Great idea. We'll be wanted for something else," Luke said sarcastically.

We stood there, thinking for a minute. I started to say we should do it ourselves when Luke snapped his fingers. "Got it! My uncle is a retired doctor. I'll ask him to do it," he said excitedly.

"He won't be suspicious?" I asked. I didn't want anyone calling the cops on us for something as simple as getting blood drawn.

"No. He'll think it's cool. He's great that way," Luke assured me. "He's rather eccentric."

"Okay, whatever," I said with a shrug. An eccentric uncle didn't sound like the best option, but it was better than nothing.

"I'll be back in a jiffy!" He smiled cheerfully and headed out the hatch.

I watched him leave and looked around, unsure what to do. *I wonder if he should have gone by himself,* I thought worriedly, glancing back toward the hatch. *I guess it doesn't matter now.*

I made my way over to the door at the back of the room, surveying all the high-tech equipment as I went. *Where do they get the money for this stuff?* I wondered. *I seriously doubt Sarah or Luke is rich enough to afford all this.*

I opened the door on the back wall and stepped inside the little room. It was a mini science lab with one laptop on a rolling desk that was currently in the corner of the room. The walls were lined with cabinets and counter space, although you could hardly see the counter due to all the science test tubes, random pieces of metal, and tools scattered about.

"Whatcha doing?" I said, walking up behind Sarah. She swirled some liquid around in a test tube.

"Fixing this," she replied, nodding toward a pile of metal on the counter.

"What is it?" I asked, unsure whether that pile of metal had ever been something in the first place.

"It used to be the lock to the back door, but it malfunctioned, so we had to take it off. It broke in the process," she said. She carefully picked up the two largest pieces of metal and poured the liquid onto the place where they connected.

"What's in the jar? I'd think you'd weld this stuff together instead of gluing it," I said, watching her spread the liquid across the seam with a paintbrush.

"I'm testing this metal glue," she said, placing the paintbrush in a cup of water. "It's supposed to work just as well as if you had welded these pieces together with half the amount of work." She turned to me and smiled. "We'll have to see if this hypothesis is true."

She got back to work, and I walked around the lab, examining the works in progress. I got back to where Sarah was and asked, "So who's the scientist here, you or Luke?"

She laughed and shook her head. "Not me. Luke is definitely the scientist. I'm a mechanic and flight engineer."

"Really? I thought you told me you were a teacher," I said, surprised. *I never knew she liked mechanics*, I thought.

"Actually, I'm all three. I teach mechanics class at Truth Academy for the fourth-graders," she explained. "Alongside teaching, I fix things."

"And apparently you're a secret agent, too," I said, grinning. "I guess you're a regular renaissance girl."

She laughed again. "Then we have a lot in common," she replied.

"How so?" I asked, putting my hands on my hips.

"You're an agent, an actress—"

"Those two go hand in hand," I interrupted her.

"If you say so, but you called me an agent, and my acting skills aren't quite up to par," Sarah said, giving me a knowing look.

"Okay, fine. I'm an actress." I rolled my eyes.

"You know gadgets really well," she continued, turning back to her project. "You're a computer hacker. I could keep going on and on, you know."

"All right, so we're both renaissance girls. Who cares? That doesn't mean we have a lot in common," I retorted.

"Well, let's not forget we're completely identical. You should have been at Mom's family reunion last year. Everyone thought I was you," Sarah said with a smile.

"I'm sure that was pretty funny," I agreed.

"And the other day I went to the Patrick Brian's Power Company site for a tour. I went as a teacher, pretending I was taking a pre-tour so I could bring my class later." Sarah put her project down and turned back to face me. "It was so funny! Someone came and asked if I'd dyed my hair," she said, grinning at me.

"Seriously?" I asked. Suddenly Mr. Brian's questions about me being at work on my day off made so much more sense. "You were there? When?"

Sarah's smile faded to concern. "Yesterday, not long before Luke brought you here. Why?"

"Because I almost got fired for spying on Mr. Brian during one of his meetings," I cried. "Luckily I'm a good actress so he fell for my story."

"Oh, I had no idea. I'm so sorry. I just wanted to get a feel for the layout of the place," Sarah apologized.

I sighed. "I guess it doesn't matter now. He believed my sock story." I shook my head. *Another way Sarah has messed things up for me*, I thought angrily.

Sarah looked at me thoughtfully. "You know," she said, "if we look so much alike that people mistook me for you despite the different hair color, I could totally fake being you. You could be in two places at once."

I nodded. "That's true. I could be at Mr. Zaiden's while you are at Mr. Brian's, and they'd never know. Both men think I don't have any family."

"That's perfect!" Sarah said, getting excited. "That totally makes things easier."

Just then we heard the hatch opening. "Must be Luke," I said, walking out of the science lab. "That didn't take too long." Sarah followed me.

Luke closed the hatch and jumped off the ladder as we walked over to him.

"Oh, Luke, you look ... terrible," Sarah said, biting her lip.

"Thanks," Luke replied, grinning half-heartedly. He looked rather pale.

"I knew it. You shouldn't have trusted your uncle to do this," I said, crossing my arms.

"Yeah, he's a little more out of it than I thought," Luke said. "I'm glad he actually had the right equipment. Oh, and luckily he doesn't live far from here, so I didn't have to drive lightheaded for too long. Anyways, I got the blood you wanted." He handed me a plastic bag containing blood.

Sarah looked like she was going to faint. "I'll be in the lab if you need me," she said and hurried off.

I pulled a chair over for Luke and made him sit down. "You rest while I get things ready to go," I said. I got a piece of paper and some fingerprint powder. After getting Luke's fingerprint, I looked around for a cloth. "Got any bandanas or old T-shirts around here?" I asked.

"Yup. That plastic bucket has lots of old rags in it," Luke answered, pointing to the top shelf.

I grabbed the bucket and pulled out the newest-looking rag. Emptying the bucket of the other rags, I placed the rag at the bottom and poured the bag of blood over the top. The rag soaked it up quickly. "Here we are," I said, showing Luke my work.

"Perfecto," he said, grinning at me. He was looking less pale and more like himself.

I checked my watch. It was nine thirty. "It's pretty late. I'd better call Mr. Zaiden and see if he's home."

"You'd better call from your house, just in case he tracks

where the call comes from," Luke warned. "Do you think he'll want the evidence tonight?"

"Most likely," I replied. "So I'd better get going."

"All right. See you tomorrow," Luke said with a yawn.

I got all my stuff together and headed for the ladder, when Sarah ran out toward us. "Guys! We need to get this on the news," she said excitedly. "If you want this to be super official, put it in the newspaper. Your boss will surely see it then, and he'll have to believe you."

"Do you know of a way to do that?" Luke asked.

"And you'd need a picture of Luke in the paper," I said. "I'm not sure it would be a good idea."

"Leave this to me. I'll make it work," she said, smiling confidently.

I felt nervous trusting her with this task, but I didn't see any other options. "All right. I'll be looking for the story in the paper." I started to climb out of the hatch when I remembered an important detail. "Luke, you can't step out of this building without a disguise on."

Luke gave me a thumbs-up. "I'll find something."

"It had better be excellent!" I replied.

I rushed home and called Mr. Zaiden.

"Hello, Richard Zaiden speaking," he said in his usual business answer.

"Hey, this is Mariah. Are you still at work?" I asked.

"I'm on my way out the door. Why? Do you have something for me?" he said curiously.

"I did what you asked," I said, faking disgust. "I'm not happy about it."

"Good work! I assume you have evidence for me?" he asked suspiciously.

"Yup. Want me to bring it over now or tomorrow?" I asked.

"Tomorrow morning, six o'clock. Got it?" he said sternly.

"Yes, sir," I replied. "See you then." I hung up quickly.

🔫

I got up early the next morning, got my disguise ready, and ate a quick breakfast before hurrying out the door. I carried a briefcase with me this time instead of my usual purse so my "evidence" would be safe.

I got to Mr. Zaiden's office at 5:45, but I figured he'd be there already anyways. I slid my security card through the front gate entrance and hurried to the building. As I walked, I noticed a large warehouse on the other end of the property that hadn't been there before. *I wonder why he put that in,* I thought suspiciously. *You're early. You might have time to see what's in that shed,* I thought.

I glanced up at Mr. Zaiden's office window. I didn't see any light coming from it. *Let's go for it,* I thought. I crept over to the new building. It was made of metal, with a large sliding door on the side. It looked just like Mr. Zaiden's hangar for his jet, but that hangar was about a mile from the office.

I pushed a button on my watch and sent a voice message to Luke. "If you have time, see if Mr. Zaiden's jet hangar is still at the original address," I said as quietly as possible and sent the message.

I spotted a small door next to the sliding door. It was locked with a keypad, so I decided to look for another entrance. I jogged around to the back side of the building and found part of the wall tarped over since it was still under construction.

My watch beeped. I looked down and read Luke's answer. "There's a hangar with a private airstrip behind the old martial arts building. Is that it?"

I sent a quick yes and slid under the tarp and into the hangar. I didn't see any signs of a security system being put in except for the keypad at the door, so I decided to take a look around. There were a few toolboxes here and there and some pieces of metal, which I assumed were for finishing the building. In the center of the hangar stood a large object covered by a tarp. All I could see were the wheels.

I walked over to the object and lifted the tarp. Underneath was a machine, about the size of the popular personal aircrafts. "Wow," I breathed, realizing what this machine was. "This is an EMP weapon!" I cried, amazed to see one in real life.

The door slammed. I looked up to see Mr. Zaiden walking toward me. "Yes, it is an electromagnetic pulse weapon. I'm glad you know your weapons," he said, grinning.

"This must be the latest technology," I said, still marveling. "I've never seen one in person, but I know enough to know that this baby could do a lot of damage."

"You're absolutely correct," Mr. Zaiden said with a nod. "I meant to show you this myself, but it seems your curiosity got the best of you." He cocked his head at me. "Am I right?"

I shrugged. "I didn't break in or anything. The tarp was wide open," I stated, motioning to the unfinished wall behind me.

"Oh, I know. I meant to have that wall finished and the security system set up in here before you got back, but you finished your job faster than expected," Mr. Zaiden said as he looked around the room. I was surprised that he thought I'd gotten the job done fast. *I took forever thinking of a plan*, I thought, but I put on a confident face.

"Let's go to my office," Mr. Zaiden said.

When we arrived, I set the briefcase down on his desk. "Here you go," I said, taking a deep breath.

He opened the briefcase and surveyed the contents. He nodded, picking up the paper and the rag, and finally said, "Very good." He picked up a newspaper next to him. "I see here the story of what happened. You did a good job. The police assume it was an accident."

I let out a sigh of relief. "Good," I said, sitting in the chair opposite Mr. Zaiden. "And for the record, I'm not doing that again." I crossed my arms and glared at him defiantly.

"We'll see about that, but at the moment we need to discuss some other important matters. I need you to install the security system in the hangar. Under no circumstances are you allowed to touch the EMP. Do you understand?" Mr. Zaiden asked sternly.

"Yes, sir," I replied. "But why do you have an EMP?"

"Curiosity killed the cat, young lady," Mr. Zaiden said with a fierce glare. "If you do as I say, all will be revealed shortly. You just need to trust me. Now get to work on the security."

I nodded and left the room. I got the security for the EMP hangar set up and operating by noon, all except for the camera to go in the corner next to the wall that wasn't up yet.

As I went home for lunch, Mr. Zaiden's words ran through my head. "You just need to trust me," he'd said.

Everyone keeps telling me to trust them. How can I trust anyone? Everyone keeps letting me down. What's the point of trusting in people when they let me down? I wondered.

🔫

After lunch I went to work at the PBPC. It was uneventful, and afterward I made my way to Luke's office. I got there the same time Sarah did.

I waved at her, and she smiled. "You sure look different," she said, motioning to my blonde wig.

I shrugged. "Just keeping up with the fashions, I guess," I replied jokingly.

Sarah opened the door for me, and we hurried down the stairs. After pushing the metal desk out of the way, we opened the hatch and jumped down into the computer lab.

"Hello, ladies!" Luke said, a big smile across his face. He was clearly back to normal after his blood donation. "Did Zaiden fall for my fake death?" he asked me.

"Yup, but remember, you cannot appear in town looking like you. I hope you're good at disguises," I answered.

"Well, I don't have a lot of practice, but I happen to know an expert at disguises," he said, grinning at me. "We shouldn't have any problem with that." We all walked over to the computers, Sarah sitting down at a computer and Luke and I leaning against the desk.

"What about the newspaper article? Did it work?" Sarah asked, smiling hopefully.

"Yup. I think it helped convince Mr. Zaiden," I replied. I hated to admit it, but for once Sarah had actually helped.

"So why'd you ask about the jet hangar?" Sarah asked, changing subjects.

"Oh that. Mr. Zaiden just built another hangar on his property, almost exactly like his old one," I replied. "But guess what I found inside."

"An SR-71 blackbird!" Luke suggested excitedly.

"Uh, no. What would he do with a blackbird?" I said, putting my hands on my hips.

"Spy on people, but he probably couldn't use it anyways. Those things are ancient," Luke agreed. "But it would still be super awesome."

"No, he has a giant EMP weapon," I cried.

Luke and Sarah's mouths dropped open. "No way!" they said in unison.

"That's bad," Sarah said, making a face.

"Are you kidding me? That's awesome! Did you touch it?" Luke asked, his face lit up with enthusiasm.

"Of course I did. It's the latest technology. I've never seen one so advanced. It could do a lot of damage," I said, nodding.

"How big was it?" Sarah asked as she began typing on her computer.

"About the size of a personal aircraft," I replied.

"Maybe a little more specific. A four-person or eight-person aircraft?" Sarah asked.

I thought for a moment. "I think probably an eight-person size," I replied.

Sarah clicked around for a moment and asked, "Is this it?" She turned the screen so we could see a picture of a large, high-tech EMP weapon.

"Just like it," I replied.

"This could cause mass destruction," Sarah said, turning the screen back toward herself. "The stats on this thing say you could put the whole US out of power if you did it right. It's not exactly legal for Mr. Zaiden to have one."

"And it's not legal for him to be an assassin. What's new?" Luke said, shrugging. "But what would he want an EMP for?"

"He also wanted those US security documents I photographed for him, and he wants to take over the PBPC," I added.

"Security, power companies, and EMPs. I wish we knew what he was up to," Sarah said.

"Those three go hand in hand," Luke pointed out.

"True, but that doesn't tell us what Mr. Zaiden is up to," I replied.

We were silent for a moment, and then it hit me. "I have an idea!" I said, snapping my fingers. "We need to help Mr. Zaiden take over the PBPC."

"Seriously?" Luke said, wide eyed. "You want to help an assassin further his plans?"

"Well, that's what he'll think I'm doing. He told me that he'd reveal his plan to me later as long as I help him. If I help him do this part of his plan, then we'll know what he's up to and be able to stop him," I said excitedly.

"That sounds rather risky. What if he doesn't give you enough information about his plan? Then he might be able to go through with the whole thing," Sarah argued.

I rolled my eyes. *Working with you two is a risk, too,* I thought, annoyed by my sister's cowardice.

Luke rested his chin in his hand, thinking. Finally, he said, "We really don't have a choice. We could turn him in for having an EMP, but that means Rebecca gets caught because her fingerprints are on it."

"And we really need to know more about this plan. What if Mr. Zaiden has other people he's working with on this project?" I said, hoping Sarah would agree.

Sarah sighed and spoke slowly. "Well, I guess we'll have to take the risk then."

Within an hour, we'd come up with a basic plan of attack. "I think this might work," Luke said, nodding with satisfaction.

"It *will* work," I corrected him. "It needs to work."

"So you'll work on convincing Mr. Zaiden that now is the

best time to take over the PBPC. Meanwhile you also need to make the PBPC look bad in the eyes of the public. Will you have time to keep up with both?" Sarah asked, looking slightly concerned.

"Of course I can," I replied emphatically. I felt like saying, *I'm the experienced agent, here!* But I kept my mouth shut.

"No offense, but Sarah's right," Luke said. I started to protest, but he quickly continued. "This is going to take a lot of work. We need to make sure it's flawless. You and Sarah are identical twins. You help Sarah learn how to be Amelia, and you work on being Mariah."

"I don't know about that," I said, glancing at my sister. She'd already said she wasn't the best actress. How could I know she'd do a good job?

There was an awkward silence, and finally Luke said, "Rebecca, you can't do this alone. We're willing to help you. And the two of us can't pull off this job ourselves either. We need your help just as much as you need ours. We'll help you, and you'll help us. What do you think?"

I stared at the two of them. Sarah smiled slightly, though I could tell she was nervous. Luke stared at me intently, his face completely serious and sincere. I almost agreed, but then I remembered what Mr. Zaiden had said. "You just need to trust me." *How do I know who to trust?* I thought, feeling frustrated. *Mr. Zaiden himself said he could easily dispose of you and train someone to take your place. How can you trust someone like that?*

I looked down at the ground, trying to think. *But can I really trust these guys? They were spying on me.* "Will you trust us?" Luke asked. I looked back up and met his gaze, which was completely sincere. *You have to decide right now. Either way, you're taking a risk. So who will you trust?*

Taking a deep breath, I nodded. "Okay, I'll let you help me," I said with a sigh.

Luke smiled and said, "Thanks."

Sarah gulped. "Okay, I think it's time for some acting lessons," she said, smiling sheepishly.

"You might be here a while," Luke said jokingly. Sarah elbowed him, rolling her eyes. Luke just laughed.

I smiled too and thought, *Maybe we can do this. I think I made the right choice.*

CHAPTER 8

"Beep, beep!" my watch sounded, waking me up. I read the message from Sarah.

"Almost to your apartment. Five minutes," it said.

I sent a quick "Okay" and hopped out of bed. It was an earlier morning than usual, but it was necessary so I could help Sarah get ready for her part as "Amelia." It had been three days since we'd made our basic plan of attack, each day full of my usual day's work and the evenings full of training Sarah to play "Amelia." I just hoped the acting lessons would pay off.

I had finished getting dressed when I heard a knock at my door. I went over and looked through the peephole; it was Sarah.

"Hi!" Sarah said excitedly as I opened the door. The night before I'd given her one of the office outfits I wore at the PBPC, which she now wore.

"Lookin' good," I said, grinning.

"Thanks. Now I just need to wear a wig," Sarah replied, following me into the kitchen.

"Make yourself some toast while I do my hair. Then I'll help you," I said and hurried into the bathroom to transform myself into "Mariah."

A few minutes later, my hair was red, and I began to turn Sarah's brown hair blonde. As I did Sarah's hair, I reviewed what she needed to do that day. "Always start and end the day with a security check. Make sure everything's running smoothly and that no one's hacked security. If anything is wrong, report it to Mr. Brian, unless of course it's something we're working on," I said as I pinned Sarah's wavy hair to the top of her head.

"And if one of us is working on finding information, my job is to cover up your work and make it look like nothing happened," Sarah added. "I think we've been over this a thousand times." She sighed and made a face.

"I don't care if you think it's boring. You need to know how to do my job to perfection. Otherwise Mr. Brian will know something's up," I warned. "He's rather suspicious of everyone, so he'll be watching you closely." *He'll be watching especially close after that awkward sock story*, I thought, frustrated.

"Your right," Sarah said, shrugging. "I just wish you had a less complicated job. I'm not the computer expert you are."

"Working at the PBPC is my easy job," I replied as I pinned the last piece of Sarah's hair. I grabbed the blonde wig from off the floor. "Working with Mr. Zaiden is much harder. He's a professional assassin, hacker, robber. And he can read people very well. It's much more stressful working with him than with Mr. Brian," I said, pinning the wig to Sarah's head.

"I don't know how you do it. And he still thinks you're Mariah. You've outsmarted the pro," Sarah said, giggling.

"No kidding," I said, grinning. "It's tough outsmarting the best of the best."

"I guess that makes you a pro," Sarah replied. She got up and looked at herself in the bathroom mirror. "Wow, I look super different!"

"You're now Amelia, except your eyebrows," I said, grabbing my temporary dye from the counter. I quickly dyed her eyebrows blonde and surveyed my work. She looked just like me when I played the part of Amelia.

"This is almost creepy how different I look," she said, tilting her head back and forth.

"You'll get used to it after a while. Now," I said, changing subjects, "do you have all your nondetectable equipment on you?"

"Yes, ma'am," Sarah replied, giving me a thumbs-up.

"Including the earpiece?" I asked to make sure.

"Yes," Sarah answered.

"Good. Remember, Luke will be monitoring both of us. Since I'll be at work too, you'll have to follow Luke's instructions, okay?" I asked, feeling less confident than usual. I wasn't sure how well Sarah would do being me. "If you ever have any questions or don't know what to do, ask Luke."

"Got it," Sarah said, looking at her watch. "I think it's time to go to work."

We both headed out the door and went our separate ways. Soon I arrived at Mr. Zaiden's office building. I ran into Lisa on my way upstairs.

"What are you doing here?" she asked, raising an eyebrow at me. "Aren't you working at the PBPC today?"

"Only this afternoon. Right now I need to talk to Mr. Zaiden. It's urgent," I said and tried to walk around her.

"Hold it, missy. Mr. Zaiden is attending an online conference," Lisa said, smirking at me. "You'll just have to wait."

"Okay, whatever," I said and pushed past her up the stairs. "She's annoying," I muttered. Lisa seemed to always be trying to best me, but she never could due to her laziness. *Well, if we're* able to stop Mr. Zaiden, then I won't have to work with her anymore. That's a plus, I thought.

I reached the top floor and walked over to the office door. I could hear Mr. Zaiden talking with someone. I sent Mr. Zaiden a quick message on my phone, telling him I needed to talk with him. He replied promptly, "In a conference meeting. Work on paperwork until I'm available."

I guess Lisa was right, I thought as I shrugged and put my phone back into my purse. As I turned away from the door, I heard Mr. Zaiden say my name. I turned back, thinking he was now available but then realized he was still talking to someone. I leaned against the wall and tried to act nonchalant as I listened.

"... has excellent work. If all goes according to plan, we should be ready within the next two months," Mr. Zaiden was saying. The other person replied, but I couldn't hear what he or she said. I pushed the record button on the special earrings Luke had given me and pulled out my phone, pretending to read messages as I continued listening.

"Yes," Mr. Zaiden said, his voice completely serious and proper. "We have that built." The other voice said something, and then Mr. Zaiden said, "Of course, Max. Everything is running smoothly. Things are already in motion. Now, is there anything else you need to know?"

I could tell the conversation was wrapping up, so I slowly walked over to the stairs and began walking down. I turned off the recording setting on my earrings and put my phone away. I hurried to my office and began working on paperwork. As I did so, I thought about what I'd heard. Mr. Zaiden had always seemed like he worked alone and was his own boss, but with the way he had spoken to that other person in the meeting, it sounded as though he were speaking with his superior. *Strange*, I thought, then continued working on paperwork.

Spying further on Mr. Zaiden would be risky, and at this point I couldn't afford any more risks.

"Mariah, please come to my office," Mr. Zaiden's voice boomed through the intercom.

I clicked the button. "On my way, and please turn yourself down. All of Seattle could probably hear you," I said sarcastically.

I hurried back upstairs and walked through Mr. Zaiden's open office door. "You wanted to speak with me?" Mr. Zaiden asked, leaning back in his chair.

"Yes, sir," I said, taking the seat across from him.

"About what?" Mr. Zaiden asked, tilting his head.

"The PBPC. You've said for a while that we should take it down, and I think now is the best time," I said, sitting up confidently.

"Really? And why is that?" Mr. Zaiden asked, raising an eyebrow. I then realized that I was being a little more straightforward than usual, but I couldn't help that. I'd just have to cover for it.

"Mr. Brian is having some security troubles. He's pretty stressed and not paying as much attention to all the details. He's trying to get more supporters and such, so I think he's going to be expanding the company," I explained, leaning forward.

"Why is that important?" Mr. Zaiden asked. He kept a straight face, but I could see a hint of satisfaction in his eyes. He was obviously pleased.

"Expanding the company creates stress and more security flaws. More things go overlooked because the company is distracted by bigger issues. That gives us a way in and out without being as noticed. Mr. Brian will be sunk, and he won't know what hit him," I replied.

Mr. Zaiden nodded. "Sounds like a good idea, but it's much harder to put into action," he said, crossing his arms. "I don't know if it would be a good time for me to expand my business. As you said, it's easier to get past security as you expand."

"That's why you have me," I replied, grinning. "I am, after all, the security expert at the PBPC. If you take over that building, I'll have it completely secure when you move in."

"True, but it's still rather risky. I'm not sure about your idea. You seem eager to help me further my plans," Mr. Zaiden said suspiciously. "Why the rush?"

"The sooner I help you, the sooner I get to learn how to operate the EMP," I replied confidently.

"Did I ever say I'd let you operate the EMP?" Mr. Zaiden asked, raising his eyebrows.

I shrugged. I kept up my confident act, trying to suppress my worry over the assumption I'd just made. "Well, knowing you, I just assumed you might need a little help with it. We both know tech stuff isn't your expertise."

Mr. Zaiden laughed. I was worried he was laughing at me, but I kept a confident face. He finally calmed down enough to speak. "Well, I love it! I'm glad you're excited about the learning opportunity. I'll consider your offer. Now, you'd better get going, or else you'll be late at the PBPC."

"Yes, sir," I said, standing. I couldn't help but grin as I left the room.

After going home and changing back to my normal self, I hurried to Luke's office. Down in the computer lab, we began working on our plan.

"What did Zaiden say about helping us?" Luke asked. He

stood next to his computer projection system, monitoring the PBPC and Sarah's work.

"Well, he said he'd consider it, but he's not sure," I replied.

"We have to make him sure then," Luke said, crossing his arms. "If we weaken the PBPC, it will make it easier for Mr. Zaiden to say yes."

I nodded. "But how? We don't want to get caught in the process."

We brainstormed ideas, trying to come up with a solid plan. Our original plan was to let Mr. Zaiden do the work for us, but since he hadn't jumped on board with our idea, we'd have to start the project ourselves.

Luke pulled out a box of doughnuts and started snacking. *He must have a high metabolism to be able to eat so many doughnuts and still be that skinny*, I thought.

"You know, I fing de bef fing a do," he began, his mouth full of food.

"Don't talk with your mouth full," I said, rolling my eyes.

Luke nodded and gave me a thumbs-up. He swallowed and said, "Right. Sorry."

"All right, continue. The best thing to do is what?" I asked.

"The best thing to do is send information about Mr. Brian's interactions with his customers to one of his customers. We let them know how he's been stealing extra money from them, and they'll panic. It's perfect," Luke said excitedly, doing a fist pump.

"Sounds perfect, but it isn't really," I replied, putting my hands on my hips. "I did that once, and you know how that turned out."

"Oh, yeah. That's when you fired me."

"Exactly. It's risky."

We brainstormed some other ideas but kept returning to the same one.

"We can do it!" Luke said, slapping his hand down on the table. "You just need a little bit more faith in yourself and in our team."

I have faith in myself. I'm just not completely sure about this team, I thought.

"Can you work on the project from here?" Luke asked, motioning toward all the computers lining the wall.

"Probably," I said with a nod. "The only concern I have is, what if they try to track us? They'd find your hideout, and then our operation would be blown."

"This is why Sarah is pretending to be Amelia right now. She can cover up your work as you do it," Luke said, grinning.

"She doesn't have much experience in this kind of work," I argued.

"No, but I do. I can walk her through it," Luke replied, standing up extra straight.

I thought for a moment, then shrugged. "If you think you can do it, then let's go for it."

"No problemo," Luke said with a salute. "This will be a piece of doughnut."

I rolled my eyes. "You're obsessed with doughnuts," I said and walked over to one of the computers against the wall. I sat down and got to work.

r

"All right, it's sent," I said a few hours later. I'd gotten the info I'd needed and sent it to Mr. Brian's largest customer through a hidden e-mail. Now we just needed to wait.

"Good. Sarah just finished covering our tracks. I think we can call this mission a success," Luke said, grinning at me.

"We'll know by tomorrow," I said, standing up and stretching. I glanced at the time on the computer. "It's just about dinnertime. Sarah should wrap things up and get going."

"Hey, Sarah, you'd better finish up and leave," Luke said into his earpiece. A few seconds later, he turned to me. "She says she's almost done. It'll be another fifteen minutes probably."

"If she doesn't leave soon, Mr. Brian may get suspicious," I warned.

Fifteen minutes later Sarah said she was getting ready to go. "Does Mr. Brian know she's still there?" I asked.

Luke relayed my question, and then said, "She's not sure. Does she need to talk to him?"

I bit my lip, not sure what to do. If Sarah told him she was leaving, he'd ask why she was there late. If she didn't tell him, would the guard tell him she'd left late? Which was the better option? "I guess ... I guess she can just leave," I said hesitantly.

Fifteen minutes later Sarah showed up at the computer lab. "Hey, guys!" she called, climbing down the ladder. It was weird seeing her as Amelia. It felt like I was looking at myself.

"How'd it go?" Luke asked.

"All right, I think. Everyone thought I was Amelia," Sarah said, smiling. "But man, that was a long day's work. I think I prefer teaching." She smiled at me, looking a little exhausted.

"Well, it was a good day's work," I said, glad no one had discovered her facade.

"Thanks," she said. "Now I need to get this wig off."

"And I need to get home," I said. I helped Sarah take the wig off and put it in my purse. Then I headed home.

The next morning I headed to the PBPC, ready for work. I didn't need to go to Mr. Zaiden's office, so Sarah didn't have to take my place.

I sat at my desk, going through routine security checks, when I heard Mr. Brian yelling, and he wasn't yelling through an intercom. *Oh, boy. I think our plan just officially worked*, I thought. I continued working as usual, making sure security was functioning properly.

It wasn't long before Mr. Brian called my name through the intercom. "Amelia, get to my office right now!" he screamed.

"On my way," I replied and hurried to his office. I opened the door and said, "Yes, sir?"

"Sit down," he said, angrily waving toward the chair. I sat down and waited for him to speak. "I am very disappointed in you," Mr. Brian said, glaring at me.

I raised an eyebrow. "Why?" I asked, trying to look confused.

"You should know why! We've been having all these security problems—people giving away information, someone breaking into the lab downstairs, and on and on and on," Mr. Brain cried as he paced the room. "And you keep on 'fixing' things, only to find that we have more security breaches."

"I ... I'm sorry sir, but I can't make everything perfect," I said quietly. "I've been doing my best."

"Well, it hasn't been good enough!" he yelled, slamming his fist on his desk. "I've had enough patience with you, and I'm done!"

"Done?" I asked, my eyes widening. "Sir, I don't understand," I said, but inside I did understand.

"Young lady, you've caused too much trouble. You're fired!" Mr. Brian shouted, his eyes blazing with rage.

"But sir, haven't I done a lot of good for you? You can't just fire me," I argued, but his mind was obviously made up.

"It doesn't matter. You're fired, and that's that. Now pack up your stuff and go!" Mr. Brian roared. He opened the door and waved for me to leave.

"You'll regret this. You won't find a security computer tech person like me again," I said, standing up and facing Mr. Brian. I tried hard to keep my face calm and confident, trying to hide my fear.

"I don't care. Just get out of here in the next thirty minutes! Do you understand me?" Mr. Brian glared intensely at me.

"I understand. Thank you for the opportunity to work with you," I replied sarcastically and marched out of his office.

Thirty minutes later I stood outside the PBPC with all my equipment, waiting for Luke to pick me up. "Where is he?" I muttered. I wondered whether he was still working on his disguise since I'd told him to pick me up while looking like a different person. *I just can't believe this*, I thought, still in shock. *How could Mr. Brian just fire me?*

A few minutes later, Luke's car pulled up. He got out and opened the trunk for me. Luke's normally brown hair was black with red, green, and blue stripes in front. He wore dark sunglasses, and his outfit made him look like a gangster. I put my stuff in the trunk and climbed into the passenger seat of the car. "Thanks for the ride," I said to my gangster driver.

"No problemo," Luke replied, giving me a thumbs-up. He drove me to my apartment and helped me take all my stuff inside.

"I just can't believe this," I said, bringing the last few things inside.

"I know. Me neither. You had a lot more stuff at the PBPC than I expected," Luke said, setting down my laptop from work.

"No, I mean I can't believe it. I ... I got fired!" I cried, not sure what to do. I felt like crying. I crossed my arms and plopped down in a chair. "Now what are we going to do?" I asked, more to myself than to Luke.

"Keep going," he answered. He sat down on the couch and smiled at me. "God causes all things to work together for good. We just have to have faith."

"Well, I don't think faith is going to help us. I just got fired! Mr. Zaiden is gonna kill me when he finds out," I said, realizing just how serious a blow this was. "We'll never make it," I muttered, fear gripping me.

"We can do this," Luke said, nodding firmly. "It'll work."

"Yeah, because 'God causes all things to work together for good.' Right. That totally worked when I was a kid, so it'll totally work now," I replied sarcastically. I pulled my blonde wig off my head and threw it on the floor.

Luke was quiet for a moment, his expression serious now. He nodded. "Things probably didn't seem so great when your parents got divorced or when you moved to Seattle and your dad didn't really care about you, huh?"

His question caught me off guard. I expected another sermon, not sympathy. "Not really," I replied.

"You got a job working for two bad guys, one who steals money from his customers and one who's a retired assassin. That's pretty bad too, huh?" Luke asked. This time he was obviously trying to hide a grin.

"It wasn't that bad. I gained a lot of experience."

"Not good experience, though. You could go to jail, ya know," Luke retorted. I just shrugged, since I couldn't argue with that statement. "But, if you hadn't started working for Mr. Brian and Mr. Zaiden, we wouldn't have been able to start working on our project to expose the PBPC's fraud. And if you hadn't messed up a few times in your acting around Sarah and me, then we wouldn't have learned about Mr. Zaiden, who is an assassin, and he's way more of a threat than Mr. Brian," Luke said, raising his eyebrows at me.

I sighed. Luke was right, but I didn't want to admit it. "So?" I asked with a shrug and looked out the window.

"So even though we all made some mistakes, we are making progress. We're closer to our goal than we were before, and you are now on a better track. Aren't those good things?" Luke asked, smiling a little.

"I could very well possibly still go to jail for years and years," I said angrily. "It's not like you'll have to."

"I suppose so," Luke said, nodding thoughtfully. "But right now that isn't our concern. We need to be focused on destroying the bad stuff going on around us."

I sat silently, thinking. *Luke's right, but I sure have a lot more on the line than he does. It's not worth the risk,* I thought. My mind argued with itself, half of me saying I should give up but the other half of me knowing that wasn't the right thing to do. *You got into this mess. You've got to fix it,* I told myself. I took a deep breath and said, "You're right. Let's get to your office and get to work."

Luke grinned. "That's the spirit! Let's go!" he said.

🔫

Back at Luke's office, we began working on a new plan, since our old one would no longer work now that Mr. Brian had fired me. "We could just wait and see what happens with the info we sent to Mr. Brian's customer," Sarah suggested.

"I'm not sure if that will be enough, though," I said, shaking my head. "Mr. Brian's covered for this kind of slipup before."

"Is there a way to prove that the false records are false? Like, can you prove they were tampered with?" Luke asked.

I thought for a moment. "I think so, but it would take a lot of time. Because no one can cover for me at the PBPC while I hack from here, we have a higher chance of being discovered," I explained.

We were talking over several ideas when Sarah suddenly snapped her fingers. "I've got it!" she exclaimed excitedly.

"What'd you catch?" Luke asked, raising his eyebrows.

Sarah ignored his attempted joke and continued. "Daniel is a trained detective, isn't he?"

Luke nodded. "Yeah, he's helped the Oregon Police Department a lot on their cases," Luke answered.

"Who's Daniel?" I asked.

"Oh, he's one of my buddies from high school. He's super cool," Luke explained.

"So why don't we have Daniel come talk to the police here in Seattle? He can explain that he's been working undercover, via us, trying to expose the PBPC's frauds," Sarah suggested.

"He could say he's got a way to prove that the PBPC is guilty by bringing me in and working through the false records to show the real ones," I said, catching on to Sarah's idea.

"That could possibly work, except for one thing. We aren't licensed detectives," Luke put in.

"Hmm, I didn't think of that," Sarah said, pursing her lips.

"We don't have to be," I said, getting an idea. "I was just fired from the PBPC, remember? Maybe I could fake being fired for realizing about the fraud and telling someone."

"That just might work," Sarah said, nodding. "You were just an average employee who stumbled upon some evidence and told another employee who told the boss, and maybe that's why you were fired."

"It's perfect," I said confidently.

"Don't get too excited yet. I'll call Daniel and see if this idea works," Luke said, and he hurried over to his computer to make the call.

Sarah looked thoughtful. "Well, what about the fact that you worked with Mr. Brian, covering up the fraud? If he gets caught, he'll probably tell the police everything, and you'll be in trouble for helping him." Sarah looked nervous. "Maybe this isn't a good idea."

"We can probably come up with a story to cover for that for as long as we need to," I replied.

"What do you mean, for as long as we need to?" Sarah asked.

I shrugged. "Well, if our plans for catching Mr. Zaiden work, then I'm totally guilty. There won't be any reason to keep lying about my work at the PBPC. It will probably be found out eventually," I said, realizing the depth of the situation. I would be in prison forever.

I suddenly got a sinking feeling inside. *I don't want to spend half my life in jail. Maybe I could just find a way to disappear after he's caught,* I wondered but quickly brushed the idea aside. *One step at a time, girl,* I warned myself.

A few minutes later, Luke came back with an answer. "Daniel says he can do it. He's flying here now. We need to have all the evidence ready for when he gets here," Luke said.

"Let's get to work then," I replied.

"Okay, I think we have everything," Sarah said. She'd just finished helping me put all our evidence against Mr. Brian in a briefcase.

"You get the briefcase, and I'll get the laptop," I said, grabbing Luke's laptop and placing it in its case. I was again disguised as Amelia, ready to take on the task of proving Mr. Brian's guilt. *He's going down*, I told myself.

Sarah grabbed the briefcase and hurried up the ladder. I followed right behind her with the laptop. Luke had the car ready to go when we got there. "Hurry up! Daniel's gonna be waiting for us!" Luke said, grabbing the laptop from me and shoving it into the trunk.

We drove to the police station, where Daniel said he'd meet us. As we pulled into the parking lot, a young man walked toward our car. He was of average height with light-brown hair and broad shoulders. He wore sunglasses and a black trench coat, and he had a briefcase.

We all got out of the car, and the man greeted us. "Hey, guys! Nice to see you all." His voice boomed across the entire parking lot.

"Hey, Daniel!" Luke said, giving his friend a firm handshake. "Glad you could make it."

"Always ready to help a friend," he replied.

"But what's with the trench coat? We don't live in the 1950s," I said as I pulled the laptop out of the trunk.

"That's not nice," Sarah whispered, glaring at me as she grabbed our briefcase.

"I'm a detective, ma'am," Daniel replied. "This is typical detective garb."

"Or not," I said, rolling my eyes. *If that won't draw suspicion, I don't know what will*, I thought.

"Okay, I probably went a little overboard, but come on. This is my first case in weeks," Daniel said.

"Let's forget the trench coat and get inside," Sarah said, a little more firmly than usual. "It's starting to rain."

We all hurried into the police station, Daniel leading the way. After going through security, Daniel hurried up to the front desk and pulled out a badge. "My associates are now here. Would you please inform Sergeant Dalton?" Daniel said, very businesslike.

The officer asked us to show our IDs before radioing Dalton, and he then asked us to wait in the lobby. A few minutes later, a police sergeant walked into the room through a metal "Do Not Enter" door. "Sergeant Dalton," Daniel said, standing as he entered the room. "My associates I told you about have arrived."

"Very good," the sergeant said, his face and voice expressionless.

"This is Luke Mason, and this is Sarah Sanders. They're my research assistants, and this is Amelia Richards. She is a former employee of the Patrick Brian Power Company," Daniel informed the sergeant.

"Yes, nice to meet you. I'm Sergeant Dalton," the officer said.

"I think once we show you our evidence, you'll understand the seriousness of this situation," Daniel said, removing his sunglasses. Even though his costume was a little overdone, Daniel did a good job of being professional.

"Please excuse me a moment," Sergeant Dalton said and went back through the metal door. Daniel sat back down, and we waited. I began to wonder whether the officer had forgotten we were still there when he finally returned.

"Okay, your IDs check out as authentic. Please follow me,"

Sergeant Dalton said, motioning for us to follow him through the metal door. I sighed with relief. Even though my "Amelia" ID had never failed, there was always that worry in the back of my mind that it would fail me someday.

We followed the sergeant until we reached a door with a security guard standing next to it. "Please allow Officer Landon to search your briefcases before you enter. Security precautions, you know," Dalton explained.

Officer Landon waved a metal detector over the briefcases, checked the laptop to be sure it wasn't a bomb, and then nodded to the sergeant. "Okay, please come in," Dalton said, opening the door for us. Inside the room was a round conference table. "Please take a seat. Now, Mr. Daniel Reid, please explain your case," the officer said, taking his seat and leaning back in his chair. I felt like we were in court instead of at a police station.

Daniel launched into an explanation of why we were there, going through various details and materials Luke, Sarah, and I had put together against Mr. Brian. "So the evidence points toward the theft of money from Mr. Brian's clients, sir," Daniel concluded.

Dalton raised an eyebrow. "Yes, but that is not solid evidence. We can't start poking around in the PBPC without solid evidence," he said, yawning.

"I realize that, sir, and that is why Amelia is here. She is a former employee of the PBPC," Daniel said, motioning toward me.

"Mm-hmm," the sergeant said, looking over several papers we had brought. "So, Ms. Amelia, you worked in the security department of the PBPC?" he asked.

"Yes, sir," I replied.

"But you were fired this week? Why?" he asked.

"Let me explain from the beginning," I said. "You see, I do more online security than anything else. I make sure people aren't hacking into our accounts and such."

"Mm-hmm." The sergeant nodded.

"One day I was going through the usual routine system checks and came across some records that were different from the records we publish to our investors, so I looked them over. The records I found were the original records and showed an accounting of all the money that's ever been stolen. At first I thought maybe it was a mistake or something, but after reviewing more files, I found it to be real. When I mentioned this to Mr. Brian, he fired me," I concluded. The story was fake, but the evidence was real. Mr. Brian was indeed stealing money.

"If I asked you to show me these records in the PBPC computer system, would you be able to find them?" Dalton asked. He looked slightly more interested than before.

"Yes, sir," I replied confidently.

"Well, is that not why you have your laptop? Can you show us these records off-site?" the sergeant asked me.

"Yeah. Great thing is, I still have complete access to the company because they haven't taken my user code off their site yet," I said as I opened the laptop and pulled up the company's website. "All I have to do is log in and take you to the correct page," I explained, hoping Mr. Brian had overlooked removing my account when he'd fired me. Sergeant Dalton monitored my work over my shoulder. My guess was correct. My password still allowed me into the company's security system. I quickly did some hacking and found the unchanged records for the police officer.

Sergeant Dalton grabbed his radio and called another officer. "Chelsea to meeting room B. Chelsea to meeting room

B." Soon Chelsea was there, and she began intently studying the files.

"Chelsea is our computer tech. She'll be able to tell us which records are real and which are fake," Dalton explained.

After a long while of reading and looking at codes, Chelsea nodded. "Whoever did this work is good, but I'm positive that this hidden record is the real one," she said.

"Is that the evidence you need to get started on this case?" Daniel asked.

"More than enough," Dalton replied, the slightest smile showing on his face.

"Do you need any more of our services?" Daniel offered.

"We'll need these records, ma'am," Chelsea said to me.

"Of course. I'll e-mail them to you now," I said and quickly sent them.

After going over a few more details, Sergeant Dalton finally said, "Well, I think that's all then. Good work, Detective. We've been watching the PBPC closely due to complaints from investors but couldn't find any proof for our suspicions. This may be the lead we need. We'll look into it further."

"Glad to be of service," Daniel said, shaking the sergeant's hand.

"I believe you all may go now, but we may need to call you again later, especially you, Amelia, to testify in court," Dalton explained.

Daniel gave his number to the sergeant, and then we all left.

"Operation stop-the-PBPC-from-stealing-other-people's-money ... success!" Daniel cried as we walked over to our car.

"Good job, buddy!" Luke said. "That went great! I can't believe you got all that information ready to explain so fast."

"I think that was a new record," Daniel said, grinning.

"Now I'd better get home. If the officer calls me, I'll let you know and head back over this way."

"All right, see you," Luke said, giving Daniel a pat on the back.

The rest of us drove back to Luke's office. Just as we got back to the computer lab, we got a call from Daniel. Luke answered on his computer so we all could hear. "Hey, Daniel. What's up?" he said cheerily.

"Bad news," Daniel replied, his voice sounding defeated. "The police called me."

"Oh no," I moaned. *I knew our meeting with the police went too easy*, I thought, frustrated.

"What's wrong? They said we had all the evidence they needed," Sarah said, looking confused.

"They said that they checked on the PBPC records that we sent them, and they were blank. All the information we gave them got deleted somehow," Daniel replied.

"How is that even possible?" I cried, anger boiling inside me.

"Not only that, but they think we all wasted their time trying to get back at the PBPC for firing you. They said you should have called your lawyer instead of hiring a detective to try to dig up false evidence about the PBPC," Daniel said. He sighed loudly. "I don't know what to do now. I'm worried they might try to sue you."

"You're telling me that they gave up on our case because the documents we e-mailed them are blank?" Luke said. His eyes blazed, and he clenched his fists.

"Pretty much. Our case already seemed pretty small to them when I first got there. Now they think this was all a joke," Daniel said sadly. "I'm sorry, guys. I wish I could help you fix this, but they pretty much banned me from ever stepping foot in their department again unless it's because I'm being arrested."

"Wow. How rude," Luke said dramatically. "Then I guess we'll think of a new plan. Don't worry—everything will work out!" He nodded firmly and stood up straight. "Thank you for informing us of the situation, Daniel," he said professionally. "We will let you know how things turn out."

"All right. I'll be praying for you all. Bye," Daniel said, and he hung up.

"I knew he shouldn't have worn the trench coat," I muttered.

"What are we going to do?" Sarah exclaimed, sitting down in a chair. She looked ready to cry. "I thought for sure everything was going according to plan."

Luke sighed. He was obviously trying to hold himself together. "Everything will be okay. Let's just take a breather and then come up with a new plan," he suggested.

I nodded. "I think we should come back tomorrow and think of a new plan. No point working on one now. I think I'll head home. I'll see you all tomorrow," I said and left.

r

At home I changed out of my disguise, ate dinner, and then plopped down on the couch. I still couldn't believe I'd been fired. Then suddenly I remembered ... Mr. Zaiden! What would he say if he found out I'd been fired? Of all the things he'd gotten mad about before, this would be the worst.

How will I cover for this one? I thought, fear rising in me. I thought about Luke and the way he always handled everything. *Every single time he goes back to God. "God will work it all out." He's so calm about everything, even when things are going* completely wrong. I sighed. *I wish I could have that kind of faith*, I thought and shook my head. *What's the point? God failed me when I was younger, when I actually believed in Him. No point in reliving that pain*, I told myself.

I went to bed that night, my mind wrestling with the concept of God and faith. I finally drifted off to sleep, with my mind still pondering Luke's childlike faith.

The next morning I woke up early, unable to go back to sleep, knowing I'd have to face Mr. Zaiden. Somehow he always found out how my work at the PBPC went. If he already knew I was fired, then I would be in big trouble when I showed up at work.

I ate breakfast, got into my "Mariah" costume, and checked the time. I still had an hour before I needed to be at work. I decided to take a walk around town and buy myself a coffee on the way there.

Thick fog blanketed the city that morning. Not many people were out and about at five thirty in the morning. I got my coffee and slowly walked down the street, looking around at all the buildings, silhouettes in the fog.

I loved how mysterious the fog made everything look. It made me think of Sarah and me when we were twelve. On foggy days we would make up stories about detectives, using the fog to help us "detectives" slip away without being seen. Our stories usually ended up pretty wild, with make-believe car chases, injuries, and the like to add drama. *Funny how things ended up*, I thought with a smile. *We played detective yesterday, and I've been playing secret agent for two years.*

For some reason I decided to walk toward the PBPC instead

of toward Mr. Zaiden's office building. *You can't run from your problems*, I told myself, but I kept on walking in the same direction. As I neared the PBPC, I noticed flashing red and blue lights shining through the fog.

I got closer and noticed that the parking lot had been taped off with caution tape, and there were police officers milling about the premises. One officer stood by the entrance to the parking lot. "Excuse me, ma'am, but you're not allowed to cross this tape," he said, motioning for me to back up.

"What happened?" I asked, motioning toward all the police cars.

"There was a murder, ma'am," the officer replied.

"What?" I cried, shocked. "Who was killed? I mean, what happened? How ... not here ..." I started to feel lightheaded.

"Take a breath, ma'am. We don't need you fainting," the officer warned. "This is a classified case. We still don't have all the details, but if you know anything about the case, then we need you to tell us."

"I ... I don't, but I ... I have friends who work here, " I said, trying to communicate despite my shock. "Um, can you tell me who it was?"

"It's classified, ma'am," the officer replied.

"Please, sir! I need to know. My friends work here," I cried, taking a step toward him.

"Do not cross the tape!" the officer cried, holding his hands out toward me. I stopped moving, and he lowered his hands. "Look, I've never worked on a murder case before, but, well, let me talk to the lieutenant."

I waited as patiently as I could while the officer radioed the lieutenant. The lieutenant came over, and the two began talking quietly. Then the lieutenant turned to me.

"What's your name?" the lieutenant asked.

"Mariah Cadman," I replied, knowing it wasn't my real name, but I didn't have any other choice. I was completely disguised as her, so I couldn't say I was Amelia or Rebecca.

"You said you have friends who work here?" he asked.

"Yes, sir," I replied.

"Were you around here this morning at five?" the lieutenant asked.

"No, sir. I was at home eating breakfast," I answered truthfully.

"So you have no idea what happened here?" the lieutenant asked. I could tell from his expression that they didn't have many clues or leads.

"No," I replied.

"When were you at the PBPC last?" he asked.

"Yesterday morning," I replied, impatiently waiting for them to tell me who had been murdered. "Can't you just tell me what happened?"

"No, I can't. We aren't even sure ourselves," the lieutenant replied. "All we know is that we got a call from one of the employees here who showed up to find the body."

"Whose body?" I asked, about ready to scream.

Another officer walked up at that moment and began talking to the lieutenant. After a moment the lieutenant turned back to me. "Look, this is a very serious matter. I'm sorry, but I can't tell you at this moment."

"Yes, you can. You're just choosing not to!" I cried. I felt ready to explode.

"I'm sorry, ma'am. When we have enough information, you'll probably hear about the incident on the news. Good day," the lieutenant said and walked away, shaking his head.

The other officer smiled weakly at me. "Sorry. I wish I could help you," he said apologetically.

"No, it's okay," I said. "Um, I was here yesterday morning. If you need me to tell you anything about yesterday morning, I can, but I don't think that will be much help." My voice trembled from shock.

The officer got my phone number, then said, "We'll contact you if we need to. Have a nice day."

I frowned and walked away. I looked down at my watch. Six o'clock in the morning. I pressed a few buttons and called Luke with my watch.

"Good morning! How can I help you?" he asked cheerily.

"It's not a good morning," I said, trying to hold back tears. "Someone was murdered at the PBPC, and they won't tell me who, and I'm afraid it's—"

"Whoa, girl. Take it easy. Do you have time to come to my office?" Luke asked. His voice was calm and gentle, as though he were talking to someone much younger than I. Normally this would have bugged me, but I was too upset to care.

"Maybe. I ... I'll just go to work late," I decided.

"Okay, hurry on over here," Luke said and hung up.

I walked as quickly as possible to Luke's office, glancing around me as I walked. The thought of someone being murdered where I used to work had me on edge.

Luke met me at the door and opened it for me. We hurried down into the computer lab, and Luke grabbed a chair for me. "Here you go," he said.

I sat down, and he leaned on the desk across from me. "So what happened?" he asked gently.

I explained the events of that morning and the few I got from the police. "They wouldn't tell me who. What if it was one of my coworkers? I have to know!" I felt like punching something.

"I'll see if I can find out for you," Luke replied quietly.

I sat silently for a moment, my mind whirling, and then a thought struck me. "Mr. Zaiden," I said, angrily, clenching my fists.

"What about him?" Luke asked.

"I'll bet he assassinated Mr. Brian!" I cried, slapping the chair. Rage boiled in me. "That's something he would do to get his evil plans done. I know it was him." I jumped up, ready to go confront him, but Luke pushed me back into the chair.

"Rebecca, listen to me," Luke said, keeping his hands on my shoulders, his face and voice commanding. "You are not going to go and blame your boss for murdering someone. You could be killed for doing that. You need to take a deep breath, calm down, and get back into your routine. This is not the time for being illogical."

I nodded. Luke was right. "I don't think I can go to work. I'm too ... too shocked," I said quietly.

"You'll make it," Luke replied, smiling softly. I sat there silently. After a few minutes, I took a deep breath.

"Okay. I probably need to head to work," I said, standing up.

"Before you go, can I pray for you?" Luke asked. He looked sincere, compassionate.

"Pray for me?" I asked awkwardly. Luke nodded. I thought about refusing, but the idea seemed like an okay one. It almost sounded comforting.

Luke bowed his head and began, "Dear Lord, I pray for Rebecca." He continued, but all I could think of was that someone was praying for me. "Help her to have faith," Luke prayed. "Give her strength. In Jesus's name, I pray, amen." Luke looked up at me and smiled. "You can do this," he said and gave me a hug.

I hugged him back. "Okay," I whispered.

I left the office, a little more peaceful than when I'd first arrived. Luke's prayer for me to have faith kept sticking in my mind as I walked to Mr. Zaiden's. *Have faith*, I thought. *If there is ever a time to have faith, it's now.* I walked on a little farther and finally decided to do something I hadn't done in years. *God, if You're even listening, then, well, somehow help me. Prove to me that I can have faith like Luke.*

CHAPTER 9

At Mr. Zaiden's, I found out the security was being upgraded. "What's this for?" I asked Lisa.

"Extra protection, dummy," she replied haughtily. "Now go talk to the boss. He's in his office."

"Did he ask for me?" I said, already heading up the stairs.

"Of course he did. Why else would I tell you?" she said, flipping her hair dramatically.

I rolled my eyes and hurried up the stairs to Mr. Zaiden's office. His door was open, and I walked in.

"You're late by five minutes," he stated.

"I know. Sorry about that," I said, forcing my voice to stay nonchalant. "Lisa said you wanted to talk to me." I sat down in the empty chair.

"Yes. I'll have you know that the PBPC is ours," Mr. Zaiden said, an evil grin sliding over his face.

"It is?" I asked, faking surprise. "How?"

"I assume you're thinking about the fact that you were fired. Now, I will let you know that I played a part in your being fired," Mr. Zaiden said.

"Why would you do that?" I cried. "That's cruel. Do you know how worried I was?"

"Listen to what I have to say. I had you fired because I

knew that once Brian was out of the way, the police would be checking his records. If you were still working there as Amelia, then you would be in trouble with the law," Mr. Zaiden explained.

I knew he was right. If I had still been working there, then when they handed over the company to a new boss, they would find out I'd been the one helping Mr. Brian steal money. But because Mr. Brian had fired me, I knew he would have erased any evidence of me helping him steal money. It was just his way of doing things.

Mr. Zaiden continued, "So, obviously, the best course of action was to have you fired. Now with Brian out of the way—"

"Out of the way?" I asked, pushing the record button on my earring as inconspicuously as possible.

"Yes. He's out of the way pretty much forever, just like Jason," he replied, giving me a look.

"You mean, you ... you ..." I paused, unsure whether to ask the obvious.

"Yes. Just like Jason," he replied, his evil grin growing into a smile. He sighed. "It was nice to relive the old days for once."

I felt sick to my stomach but tried to keep a confident face. "So you have a plan for taking over the PBPC after all the police work is done?" I asked.

"Yes, of course I do. But you don't need to worry about that. I have more important matters for you to work on. For now I need you to finish up paperwork and routine system checks. We'll work on our plans tomorrow," Mr. Zaiden said and dismissed me.

I hurried to my office and sat down at my desk. I pulled my earring off and held it up to my watch, waiting for it to sync. After the recording had downloaded onto the watch, I sent it to Luke.

I worked on paperwork for an hour, then stood up and stretched. My watched beeped. I looked at it and found that Luke had sent me a message. "Sorry it took so long to reply. The recording isn't enough evidence to put Zaiden behind bars," it read. "If you can get a better recording, then all we'd have to do is turn him in."

I sighed and quickly replied, "He chose his words carefully. What other evidence could I get to prove him guilty?" I sent the message quickly and sat back down.

"What are you doing?"

I jumped at the sound of Lisa's voice. She stood at my office door, her arms crossed.

"Paperwork," I replied, hoping she hadn't seen me jump.

"While you're messing with your watch? Oh, sure. I think you're up to something," she said, tilting her chin up.

I rolled my eyes. Lisa was the most annoying coworker I'd ever had. "Are watches too old fashioned for you?" I challenged.

Lisa sighed. "Whatever. All I'm trying to say is, I'm keeping my eyes on you. My eyes are on you like a hawk," she said and walked away. I turned back to my work, only to be interrupted again. "Actually, my eyes are on you like laser beams, got it?" Lisa glared at me.

I felt like laughing. "Okay, good to know," I replied. I watched her walk away and turned back to my work. *You'd better be watching her yourself,* I thought. *You don't want her spying on you or anything.*

I finished the paperwork necessary for that morning early, so I did a little snooping till I found Mr. Zaiden's secret files. I messaged Luke and asked him to run some password tests for me off-site so I wouldn't be caught breaking into the files. I decided to try the "MAX500" subfile. "Requires seventeen characters," I told Luke, "no caps." Luke asked for the instructions on finding the file and said he'd get on it.

I tried to refocus on paperwork and system checks as I waited. After an hour, I almost gave up on the idea when Luke replied, "Code: americaplanszmax1."

Glancing at the office door to be sure Lisa wasn't spying, I hesitantly typed in the code. "ACCESS GRANTED," flashed across the screen. "I'm in!" I told Luke. Inside were more subfiles.

I pulled out my flat, plastic camera and took a picture of the screen. There were files labeled "MAX budget," "MAX headquarters," "MAX power plants," "MAX America," and "MAX assignments."

What's with MAX? I wondered. I thought about it for a while and then remembered. *Max—that's who Mr. Zaiden was talking with in that online conference. But who is Max, and is this referring to him or something else?* I wanted to look at all the files and find out, but I heard footsteps coming my way. I sent another message to Luke. "Someone's coming. Erase my tracks."

A second later Luke replied, "No problemo."

I exited the screen just seconds before Lisa stuck her head into my office. "Whatcha up to?" she asked, raising her eyebrows.

"Lovely paperwork," I replied sarcastically.

"Let me see," she said, stomping into my office. She glanced over my shoulder to see a report I was writing about handling EMP weapons properly. I wrote it in code, though, and her face proved she couldn't read it. She shrugged. "Okay, cool. But remember, I'm watching."

I smiled as she left. "Have a nice day!" I said.

At noon I headed outside to go to lunch. Mr. Zaiden met me at the front gate. "Heading out?" he asked.

"Yup," I said, grinning. "And I'll have you know that all my paperwork is now up to date."

"Good," Mr. Zaiden said with a nod. "I wonder if you wouldn't mind holding off on lunch a little." He nodded toward the hangar at the back of the property. "Someone's got to learn how to run that bad boy."

Excitement bubbled up in me. Learn to use an EMP? I would miss lunch any day to learn how to use one. "I am a fast learner," I said, smiling.

"Good. Then come with me," he said. We walked over to the hangar, and Mr. Zaiden unlocked the door so we could enter.

"I see the back wall is fixed," I said with a nod.

"Yes. We don't want such a valuable weapon stolen," he replied, pulling the tarp off the EMP.

I stared in awe at the weapon. It was sleek and very high tech. The thought of learning how to use something so advanced, so cool, and—well, so expensive—made me giddy. I wanted to run my hand along the smooth metal, but I restrained myself. I knew Mr. Zaiden wouldn't want me touching such precious equipment just yet.

"It's a beauty, isn't it?" Mr. Zaiden asked, smiling. He grabbed a box of plastic gloves from off the ground and handed me a pair. "You'll need to wear these so you don't get fingerprints on this bad boy," he explained. I put them on obediently. "I've put all the research you and I have done on EMPs into this manual. Don't lose it. It took a long time to gather this information," he warned.

I nodded and took the manual from him. I flipped through the pages, noticing that there weren't a lot of how-tos inside.

"I take it you don't know how to use this machine very well, do you?" I said, looking up at Mr. Zaiden.

He shrugged. "I know as much as you know," he replied. "That's why I need your help. You're very good at figuring out these kinds of things. I think it will save me time if you learn how to use this machine."

We spent a good hour doing research and studying the EMP, taking notes on things we needed to remember and such. Eventually my stomach began to growl, and I was ready for a break. "I think I need some lunch," I said, getting up from my crouched position next to the EMP.

"Sounds good. We can work on this later this afternoon," Mr. Zaiden said. "Good work."

"Thanks," I said, smiling. As I walked out of the warehouse and toward the front gate, an odd feeling swept over me. Hearing Mr. Zaiden's praise for my work always gave me a surge of pride, but today it felt different, almost wrong. *Why would hearing an assassin say, "Well done" make you feel good?* part of me asked. Another part of me argued, *Of course it would make you feel good. He's a pro, after all, giving you a thumbs-up. Who doesn't want to hear a pro tell them well done?*

My mind kept arguing with itself as I walked to the nearest restaurant for lunch. I quickly ate a sandwich. As I grabbed my purse to head back to work, I got a call from Luke on my watch. I pulled an earpiece out from a side container in the watch and put it in my ear, amazed at how much was packed into the tiny watch. I clicked the answer button and walked out of the restaurant. "Hello?" I said.

"It's Luke. I think we've got a plan," he said, sounding excited. "Do you have time to swing by?"

I checked the time. "I think so—if it's a quick meeting," I replied.

"Okeydoke. What's your ETA?" he asked.

"Ten minutes," I replied and took off at a run for Luke's office.

"See you then," he said and hung up.

Ten minutes later I stood in the computer lab. "Okay, what's up?" I asked, out of breath.

"The perfect plan is up, that's what," Luke replied, bouncing with excitement.

"It's not the perfect plan, but it could work," Sarah put in quietly.

"Sarah found a red wig that looks a lot like yours," Luke began.

"It's of a lower quality, but if I pinned it up into a bun or something, it would look more convincing," Sarah said, picking up a red wig from the table. Its color matched the one I wore, but she was right. The quality was definitely not as good as my seventy-plus-dollar wig.

"It could work," I said hesitantly. "But what would you need it for?"

"You could keep Mr. Zaiden busy while I look around the place and search for evidence," Sarah explained.

I crossed my arms. "Not a chance. There are security cameras everywhere. Everyone would have to be blind not to notice there were two of me at the office," I stated firmly.

"Well, we could always switch places occasionally. If you find some info that you need to get back here to Luke, I could switch places with you and vice versa," she suggested.

"That sounds risky," I said, feeling unsure.

"Mr. Zaiden is getting closer to accomplishing his plans," Luke said. "You sent me that file, saying he'd killed Mr. Brian. That means he's in a hurry. We need to be ready to take risks. If we don't stop him soon, we won't be able to stop him at all."

I sighed. "So you're saying we don't have any other ideas, so this will have to do?"

Luke nodded. "Unless you have a better plan, then I say, let's go for it. I think once we get enough information against Zaiden, we can just turn it over to the police and let them handle this. It won't be as hard as we think so long as we work fast and watch our backs," he said confidently.

"We definitely have to watch our backs," I replied, thinking about Mr. Brian's assassination. I shuddered at the thought of what could happen to any of us if Mr. Zaiden found out about our plans.

Sarah placed a hand on my shoulder. "I know this is a pretty scary situation, but we need to trust God. He'll see us through," she said softly. I just shrugged, not sure whether to agree.

"Let's pray," Luke said and grabbed Sarah's hand. He held his other hand out to me. Slowly I grabbed it and bowed my head like them. "Dear Lord," Luke prayed, "we're working on this job, trying to save others from a nasty man, but we can't do it on our own. We know You are a just God. Let justice prevail so that no one else gets hurt by Mr. Zaiden. We ask for strength, and we ask for faith to believe that You are God and You are in control. Be our protector. In Jesus's name, we pray, amen."

"Amen," Sarah echoed.

I quickly let go of Luke's hand and looked down at my watch. "I need to get going," I said. "Oh, and speaking of evidence, here's my camera with the picture of the MAX500 files." I pulled my camera out of my purse and placed it in Sarah's hand.

"Okay," Sarah said and gave me a hug. I surprised myself by hugging her back.

"See you guys later," I said and waved at Luke.

As I ran back toward Mr. Zaiden's office, I thought about Luke's prayer. *We ask for faith to believe that You are God*, he'd said. *Do you have faith that God is God?* The question struck me. *Not really*, I replied, feeling almost guilty. The second half of that sentence came to mind. *Faith to believe that You are God and You are in control.*

A thought struck me again. *If you don't believe in God, how can you believe He's in control?* I shook my head and swiped my card to enter the front gate of Mr. Zaiden's office. *You can think about that later. Right now it's time to work*, I said to myself and marched back to the warehouse.

"Well, I think we should be done for the day," Mr. Zaiden said, looking satisfied.

I nodded. We'd spent several more hours working on figuring out how to use the EMP, and I thought we were pretty close to having the machine figured out. "This wasn't as hard as I'd expected," I said as we left the warehouse.

"Good thing you understand these sort of things better than I do. It would have taken me much longer all by myself," Mr. Zaiden said, smiling at me.

"Two heads are better than one," I said, grinning back.

"Be back here tomorrow morning," Mr. Zaiden said and walked toward his office building.

"Okay, see you then," I said and hurried toward the front gate. *I'm ready to head home*, I thought, feeling ready for a break. Less than a block away from Mr. Zaiden's, I ran into Sarah.

"Ready to switch places?" Sarah asked, a mischievous grin spreading across her face.

"I guess so," I replied, surveying her outfit. She wore the exact same outfit as I, and her makeup was done the same too. I just hoped the difference in our red wigs wouldn't be too noticeable.

"I'll need the security cards to get in," Sarah said, holding her hand out to me.

I placed the cards in her hand. "Okay, so if they ask you why you came back, tell them you forgot your purse in the office. My empty purse is under the desk. Grab it when you're ready to go and don't stay too long," I warned. "You don't want Mr. Zaiden suspecting that something's up."

Sarah nodded. "Got it." She took a deep breath and smiled nervously.

"Don't worry about it. You'll do fine as long as you follow the plan," I said, trying to sound reassuring both to Sarah and to myself.

"Okay, I'm going then," Sarah replied. Standing up a little straighter and with more confidence, she strode back down the street toward the office, matching her stride to my usual quick pace.

I watched her until she rounded the corner and then continued walking back to Luke's office. I got to the computer lab and found Luke eating pizza as he monitored Sarah's progress on the desktop computer.

"Grab some pizza," Luke said, motioning to the box on the chair next to him.

I pulled a chair over to the table and sat down. "How are thing's going?" I asked as I grabbed a slice.

"Good. So far no one has asked why she came back," Luke said. He was totally calm and relaxed, peaceful. *I wish I had that kind of peace*, I thought before I could stop myself.

We sat, eating pizza, for a few minutes in silence. "So,"

Luke said, breaking the silence, "I told Sarah she needed to be there for only ten minutes. Does that sound right?"

"I think so. Any longer than that, and Mr. Zaiden will start being nosy. As it is, ten minutes will make Lisa suspicious if she's there," I said, feeling a little bit nervous.

"Is she normally there in the evenings?" Luke asked, grabbing himself some more pizza.

"No, but you never know with Lisa. She's unpredictable," I replied, shrugging.

Luke checked his watch, then pressed a button on the desktop computer. "Okay, girl, get going," Luke said into the speaker.

Sarah was in my office on the computer. She logged off and bent down to grab something from under the desk. Standing up, she waved my empty purse casually as she walked out of my office. "Okay, that would be the signal. She's leaving," I said, remembering our plan.

We watched her walk out of the building and head back to the front gate. She swiped her card to leave when the guard on duty walked over and began talking to her. "Can we listen to what they're saying?" I asked, feeling nervous.

"Sure," Luke said, still totally calm. He pushed a button, and the sound turned on.

"... had to grab my purse," Sarah was saying, holding up the purse in her hand.

"Oh. That's it?" the guard asked. He didn't sound totally convinced.

"Yeah. It has my phone in it. I wasn't about to leave my phone at work," Sarah replied, her voice surprisingly full of annoyance.

"Wow. She does a good job pretending to be you!" Luke said, glancing at me.

"Whatever," I muttered, ignoring him. I continued watching Sarah.

"I need to check your purse," the guard said. Sarah sighed impatiently and handed the guard her bag.

"There had better be a phone in that purse!" I cried, worried that Sarah would be caught.

The guard held the purse for a long time. I couldn't tell whether he'd found anything inside or not. Finally, he gave Sarah the purse. "Okay, you're clear to go," he said. I sighed with relief.

Sarah said goodbye and exited through the front gate. After that we couldn't see her through the security cameras anymore.

"First day of double Mariah ... success!" Luke said, doing a fist pump.

I felt relieved. "She didn't do too bad," I said without thinking.

"Are you kidding? She did a great job!" Luke said, grinning at me. "I think this will work!"

I couldn't help but smile. Luke's enthusiasm was contagious. "Maybe," I replied.

🔫

Sarah returned, and we finalized our plans. She and I would switch on and off throughout the day, each time bringing back to Luke's office any evidence we possibly could to look through, hoping to find incriminating evidence against Mr. Zaiden. We decided Sarah should avoid Mr. Zaiden at all costs, since she didn't know a whole lot about my previous jobs with him. The fewer questions she answered about my work, the more hidden she'd be.

"Remember, if Zaiden starts picking up the pace at all, then you've got to take more risks. If need be, I can always break in and steal information," Luke said as we wrapped up our meeting.

"That would probably be a suicide mission," I said, shaking my head. "As long as this plan works, I don't think we should take any other risks."

"We could always have both of us on the premises at the same time. We'd be caught eventually, but it would be less obvious than Luke breaking in," Sarah put in.

"True," Luke agreed. We talked over a few more details, gave Sarah a few tips on her acting job, and talked strategy for finding information. "Okay, I think my brain is done thinking for the day," Luke said, yawning.

"It is getting late," I replied. "I say this meeting should be adjourned."

The next week passed. Sarah and I switched on and off, trying to gather information against Mr. Zaiden, but it wasn't working. "None of this is enough to put Zaiden behind bars," Luke said, running his fingers through his now-ruffled hair. "I've looked over all this stuff so many times, and there's nothing." He slouched in his chair and pushed the file away from him.

"At least we haven't been caught," Sarah said, trying to sound encouraging. She reached across the table from where she was sitting and picked up the file.

"We're going to all this trouble to have the two of you switch back and forth for nothing," Luke said, frustrated.

"I've learned how to run an EMP. That's something," I said half-heartedly.

"Something to further Zaiden's plans. We've got to take some more risks," Luke said, shaking his head.

"We can't take more risks," I argued. "It's not safe. We could be killed."

"No matter what we do, we could be killed. Let's go big or go home," Luke said defiantly.

"Easy for you to say. You go home to Oregon, where you'll be safe and will never have to worry about Mr. Zaiden. I go home, and I'm still working for a dangerous assassin, who could kill me whenever he wants," I said, crossing my arms.

"I wasn't serious about going home. I'm just saying that if we don't take any more risks—"

"Hold it, you two!" Sarah interrupted, looking up from the file she was holding. "I've found a common thread here."

"What is it?" I asked.

"All of these notes have different codes next to them, but some of them have room numbers. See here. There's a name from a case and then a room number," Sarah said, handing me a piece of paper. I looked it over. Next to a case name from about a year ago was a room number.

"That's my office number," I said, realizing where Sarah was going with this. "The files for this case are on my computer. It wasn't a big case, so Mr. Zaiden had me put the records into my computer to practice my coding skills."

Sarah said, "If Mr. Zaiden put room numbers for each case on here—"

"—then he probably has room numbers for the bigger stuff too," I finished. "Can I see that file?"

Sarah handed it to me, and I began flipping through it. I scanned the files for the larger cases I knew were extremely important. I found the case from when I took pictures of the government documents. "Here's one that says B108," I said and looked over more cases. Several said B108 next to them.

"Which room is B108?" Luke asked.

"That's one of the rooms in the basement. B stands for basement. Rooms 100 through 110 are all in the basement. I only have access to rooms 100 and 105," I said, flipping through several pages.

"Who has access to the other rooms?" Luke asked excitedly.

"I don't know. Room 100 is a storage room. Room 105 is one of the security rooms," I said, thinking over what I knew about the basement floorplan. "Mr. Zaiden said room 101 is where the AC system and things like that are. Nothing interesting. I've been in that room before, so I know nothings there. Rooms 102 through 104 are more storage, cleaning supplies, and stuff. Mr. Zaiden has the keys to those, but anyone can get in, if necessary."

"What about 108?" Sarah asked. "Does Mr. Zaiden ever talk about that room?"

I shook my head. "All I know is that 108, 109, and 110 all say 'Off limits' on the door. As far as I know, Mr. Zaiden is the only one who can enter those rooms."

Luke nodded, looking thoughtful. "Okay, so we need access to those rooms then."

"How?" I asked.

"Take some pictures of whatever kind of locks are on those doors and bring them to me," Luke said excitedly.

"You have an idea for an invention, don't you?" Sarah asked, raising her eyebrows.

"One I've been working on anyway," Luke said, grinning. "I think this is the perfect test for my project."

"Well, that sounds risky," I said.

"If it works, it would be a safer and faster way to get into a locked room," Luke replied mysteriously.

I sighed. "I guess I'll do that then."

"I think what we need to do is have me be Mariah all day, and you sneak around and find as much information as possible," Sarah said. "Our time is running out. Zaiden takes over the PBPC in a week. The more power he gains, the harder it will be to stop him."

"That's a dangerous plan. I say no," I said, standing up. "What will you do when Mr. Zaiden wants you to help him learn to use the EMP and all the other stuff he asks me to help with all the time? He'll know you're a fake."

"What else can we do?" Sarah asked.

"We've got to take a risk somehow," Luke put in.

I thought for a moment. "Maybe we don't have to," I replied slowly.

"What do you mean?" Sarah asked.

"I remembered that there's a computer in the security room with all the access codes on it. If I can hack into it, then I'll get access to those rooms with the real code, and the security crew will think I was allowed in," I said. *Then I won't have to worry about getting pictures of the lock for Luke's invention*, I thought.

"That sounds like a risk to me," Luke said, "but it sounds like a good idea. Let's go for it."

⌐

The next day I headed to work with Luke's new "invention" in my pocket. I told him I probably wouldn't need it, but he insisted I bring it, just in case.

I got through the front gate security just fine. Whatever

materials Luke had used to make his equipment metal detector proof amazed me. After we completed our mission, I was going to find out what it was.

I went to my office and went through usual routines of paperwork, security checks, and all the other boring stuff. I got up to head down to the basement when Mr. Zaiden knocked at my open office door. "Yes, sir," I said, turning to face him.

He raised an eyebrow at me. "I thought you were going to meet me at the EMP fifteen minutes ago," he said, sounding displeased.

I felt confused, knowing he hadn't asked me this morning to meet him there. *He must have talked to Sarah, not me,* I thought. "Sorry, I got distracted. The upgraded security system is taking time to learn, you know," I said. "I'm ready now, though."

Mr. Zaiden eyed me skeptically. He slowly replied, "Okay. Come on then."

I followed him out to the hangar as he explained what we were working on. "So we really need to develop a way to fire the EMP so people won't be able to determine where it came from," he said, trying to brainstorm ideas.

"Just fire it from your jet," I replied, thinking that answer would be simple enough.

"No, we don't have the time to create an attachment on the jet. We need to fire it from the ground," he said, shaking his head. "That's what's holding up my plans."

My eyes widened. *That's the only thing holding up his plans? Just that he doesn't know how to fire the EMP the way he wants? I* thought worriedly. *Luke is right. We really need to work fast. Faster than any of us thought.*

I spent the morning brainstorming ideas with Mr. Zaiden, using computer models to try to solve his problems. By noon we'd come up with a temporary plan Mr. Zaiden would tolerate. "For now," he said, "this will have to do. Perhaps we can think of a better plan before our deadline."

"When is our deadline?" I asked, trying to sound nonchalant.

Mr. Zaiden raised an eyebrow at me. "There is no need to be nosy, is there?" he replied seriously. I knew that wasn't really meant to be a question, so I kept my mouth shut.

"Go on back to whatever else you need to get done. Remember to get your paycheck before you leave," he reminded me.

"Yes, sir," I said and hurried back to my office. I sat down in my chair and watched the security cameras, waiting for Mr. Zaiden to go into his office. While I waited, I tried to study the lock on room B108. From what I could make out on the camera, it looked like a keypad-access, vault-style lock, so the only way of getting in would be with the code. After what seemed like an eternity, I saw Mr. Zaiden go into his office, so I grabbed my purse and headed to the basement.

I entered the security room and found one of the guards inside, watching the cameras. "Hey, Tom," I said, smiling at the bored guard.

"Hi," Tom said with a half-hearted wave. "What are you doing down here?"

"My job," I replied with a shrug.

"Still working on the new security system?" he asked.

"Yup," I said and walked over to the computer with all the security codes. I logged in as myself and clicked around at a few things, waiting for Tom to turn back to the security cameras.

After what felt like forever, Tom suddenly said, "Can you watch things for a minute? I need to get a drink of water."

"No problem," I replied and watched Tom leave. After he left, I turned back to my project. *Okay, how to find the security codes for the basement?* I thought and got to work.

A few minutes later, I found the file for the basement codes I didn't have. I clicked on file B108 to find out what the pass code was. I needed yet another code to get into the file. After several attempts to no avail, I sent a message to Luke. "Can't break code. Does the invention work on keypad-access, vault-style locks?"

A moment later he replied, "Go for it. Follow the instructions, and it should work."

I heard footsteps coming my way. I exited the computer page I was on and went to look at the security cameras. No sooner had I taken my post when Tom walked into the room. "Thanks for covering for me," he said.

"No problem," I replied sweetly. I walked back over to the security codes computer and logged out. "I'll see you later," I said to Tom, then headed out the door.

From the few glimpses of the security cameras I'd seen, I knew there was enough shadow in the basement to hide me for most of the way down the hall. I worked my way to room 108 as quietly as possible, slowly pulling Luke's invention from my pocket. When I arrived at the door, I held the pancake-sized gadget to the lock and pressed the camera button. After five seconds I pulled the gadget away and pressed several buttons on the face of the invention. I clicked "enter" and then placed the gadget next to the lock again. After a few more seconds, the machine vibrated three times. *It figured out the code!* I thought excitedly. I turned the gadget toward me and read the combination. As quietly as I could, I pressed the code into the lock. Time seemed to tick by in slow motion.

Finally, I heard the door unbolt. I pushed it open and slipped into the room.

The room had rows of file cabinets lining the walls. In the center of the room was a metal desk with a desktop computer on it; it was similar to the one Luke had but not quite as new. I took a picture of the room with my watch and sent it to Luke. Then I got to work searching.

Each file cabinet had several sets of numbers on it, which I assumed were the same numbers on the papers Sarah and I had found. I sent a quick message to Sarah. "I need case numbers," I said and waited for her response.

"Zero zero zero one one three," was her reply. I followed the file cabinets on the wall, looking for those numbers. Finally I found them. I went to open the cabinet and stopped. The lock on the cabinet was a fingerprint lock. *Are you kidding me?* I thought, frustrated with myself. *Why didn't you think of that? Good thing you brought your tools.* I pulled my toolbox out of my purse, grabbed a screwdriver, and began unscrewing the hinges from the cabinet.

Minutes ticked by. Finally, I got the door open. I reached in and grabbed file 000113 and began to pull it out. I glanced around, wondering whether moving these files would set off an alarm. I got the file completely out, then quietly pushed the door back into place and began screwing it back together.

My watch flashed. Luke sent me a message. "Sarah's headed your way to switch places. Hurry. I think Lisa's wondering where you are."

I finished getting the cabinet back in place and stuffed the file in my purse. I got up and tiptoed back to the door.

"Anyone outside the door?" I asked Luke, hoping he was monitoring the basement security and not just my office.

He quickly replied, "All clear."

I opened the door and slipped out. No one was in sight. Staying in the shadows, I made my way out of the hall and up the stairs. Reaching the first floor, I turned to walk out the door and bumped into Mr. Zaiden.

"Where do you think you're going?" he asked, his voice full of anger.

"Outside," I replied, raising an eyebrow. I hoped I sounded convincing.

Apparently I didn't. "You're coming upstairs to my office," Mr. Zaiden said sternly.

"Okay," I said, trying to sound confused.

Mr. Zaiden pushed me toward the stairs. "Get moving."

Obediently I began walking up the stairs. *Have I been found out?* I worried. I felt panicked, but I was determined to look confident despite my fear. *He probably doesn't know about the file,* I tried to reassure myself.

At the top floor, Mr. Zaiden pushed me into his office. "Take a seat," he said gruffly. There were two security guards in his office, both armed with guns.

I'm toast, I thought as I sat down.

"I'll get to the point," Mr. Zaiden said, standing in front of me. "Someone has been breaking into a lot of my files. Regularly. I have top security, the best of the best. There aren't many people I know who can break into files like that." He glared at me.

I tried to act innocent. "What kind of files?" I asked.

"Don't play games with me. These are files full of records, plans, security systems—you name it. Someone isn't being loyal. I don't tolerate traitors," Mr. Zaiden said, his evil gaze fixed on me.

"Who do you think it is?" I asked defiantly.

"Who else has the knowledge and training to do such fine

work? The only one I've given that sort of special training to, who's been trained in the mastery of hacking, breaking and entering, acting, assassination—"

"And the list goes on and on, doesn't it?" I interrupted. "Are you the one stealing the information?" I asked jokingly.

"Very funny. But you know what else I know?" he asked, sitting down on his desk.

"What?" I asked, crossing my arms.

"I know you're the best actress I've ever met, but even the best are often found out," he replied.

"What do you mean?" I asked, confused.

"Oh, you play innocent so well, yet you're anything but innocent," Mr. Zaiden said, shaking his head.

"I really don't understand what you mean," I said, raising an eyebrow. "Explain to me."

"Oh, Rebecca, if only you knew what a professional you're dealing with," Mr. Zaiden said, smiling evilly.

I froze. Rebecca? He knew my real name? But how? I took a deep breath and tried to remain calm.

"Rebecca?" I asked sarcastically. "Who's that?"

"You're so funny," Mr. Zaiden said, rolling his eyes. "You think I don't know who you are? When my files were being tampered with, I began to suspect that you were behind it. No one else here has the expertise to work so cleanly and well hidden—besides me, of course."

"Oh, so humble," I muttered, attempting to keep myself calm.

"So I asked Lisa to keep an eye on you during work, and I placed a tracking bug on you to find out some more about you. The first thing I discovered was that you don't live at the address you gave me," Mr. Zaiden said accusingly.

"Guilty as charged," I said, shrugging. "It is much safer not to reveal where you live. You ought to know that."

"The other thing I found out was that my tracking bug never followed you to the PBPC when you were being Amelia. Strange, strange, strange, isn't it?" Mr. Zaiden asked, standing back up.

"I don't get your point," I replied, confused.

Mr. Zaiden rolled his eyes. Then without warning he grabbed my wig and yanked it off.

"Hey!" I cried, both from the pain of my hair being pulled by the bobby pins and from the realization of how difficult this situation had become. I had been found out. For real.

"I'll admit, I'm impressed. You really had me going. I would never have guessed Mariah was actually Rebecca," Mr. Zaiden said, shaking his head. He pulled a small circle of metal out of my wig, a tracking bug. I started to say something, but he cut me off. "Don't try to protest. Now, please give me the files you just stole from me." He held his hand out to me.

"What files?" I said, trying to stay confident. I needed to think of a way out of this situation—and fast.

"Would you quit trying to play dumb? I know you stole them. You tripped the silent alarm when you stepped on the pressure plate, and I have video surveillance showing you did it. Now hand them over!" Mr. Zaiden cried and snatched my purse from me.

After searching through the bag, he pulled out the files and tossed my bag into his desk drawer. "Take her to the basement for now," he said to the guards.

"Yes, sir," the one on my right said, grabbing my arm. The guard on my left grabbed my other arm, and they pulled me out of my chair.

"I told you I could replace you at any time. As you probably know, it's not that hard for me to get rid of people who stand in my way," Mr. Zaiden said, glaring at me. He waved at the guards, and they pushed me from the room.

Oh, what am I going to do? I thought worriedly. As I walked down the stairs, I prayed, hoping against hope that God could possibly help me. *God, if You're even there, please help me! I'm going to die, and I don't know what to do. I need Your help.*

We descended the stairs until we reached the basement steps, where another guard wearing sunglasses stopped us. "Excuse me, but the basement is off limits," he said.

"No, it's not. The boss just sent us to take her down there," the guard on my right said, tugging on my arm. "Now let us through."

The guard blocking us didn't budge. Suddenly the guard on my right started shaking violently and then fell over backward.

"What's going on?" the guard on my left cried, but before he could draw any weapons, I punched him in the face, knocking him out.

The guard in sunglasses grabbed my arm and pulled me out the door. "Let's go!" he cried.

We ran as fast as we could to the front gate. I noticed that the two men guarding the gate were out cold.

Just outside the gate was a truck. I hopped into the passenger side.

"Hurry up!" I cried as my rescuer buckled in.

"Safety first," he replied, starting the truck. He gunned it, and we took off.

I sat there silently for a few minutes. "Thanks for coming to my rescue," I said quietly.

"You're welcome," he replied, taking his sunglasses off. "What did you think about my disguise?"

"Very well done, but where did you get the outfit?" I asked.

Luke shrugged. "When I took out the first security guard, I switched outfits with him."

"I see," I said with a nod.

"I'm glad my new Taser worked. He didn't even see it coming," Luke said excitedly.

"*I* didn't see it coming," I admitted.

Luke grabbed a small box off his belt and handed it to me. "That's the trigger. The Taser is actually on my sunglasses," he explained.

"Wow," I said half-heartedly. Though his invention impressed me, all I could think about was what had just happened. "We're doomed," I muttered.

"Did you just say we're doomed?" Luke asked, raising an eyebrow. "I don't think we're doomed. In trouble, maybe. Have no idea what to do now, maybe. But we're not doomed yet."

"Yes, we are. We've been discovered. I had what we needed in my hands, and we got caught. Now Mr. Zaiden knows who I am. We're dead!" I cried, slouching in my chair.

We both sat there silently. Suddenly I thought about my prayer and the fact that Luke had showed up just moments later. *That's called a coincidence*, I told myself. I sat silently for a moment, my mind racing. "Um, Luke?"

"That's me," Luke replied.

"How did you ... I mean why ... Why did you come to my rescue?" I asked.

He shrugged and sat silently for a moment. "Well, I saw you bump into Mr. Zaiden and then head to his office. I knew I needed to do something, so I drove over there. I didn't really have a plan. I just grabbed my Taser sunglasses and prayed God would show me what to do. I knew I wasn't going to sit around and do nothing," he said as he pulled into the parking space behind his office.

"Did ... did God really show you what to do? I mean, didn't you just come up with your plan yourself?" I asked timidly. *That was a dumb question*, I thought, resisting the urge to smack myself in the face.

Luke smiled. "Some people would try to say that I just happened to come up with the idea because my brain just comes up with crazy ideas really fast. But I would say that God answered my prayer and gave me what I needed to get the job done," he said, turning the truck off. "What would you say?"

I shrugged. "I don't know."

"But you asked the question. Why?" he asked, raising his eyebrows.

I sat silently, watching his expression. He didn't act as though he thought himself better than I. He didn't look like he was mocking me. His expression was serious, kind, compassionate ... as if he truly cared.

"I ... I asked God to save me somehow, because I didn't know what to do. I just wanted to know if He really did help me or if it was just a coincidence that you showed up," I said quietly.

"That was no coincidence. That was God!" Luke cried emphatically. He paused, then said, "I know people who would say it was a coincidence, but the more I get to know God, the more I realize that the things we call 'coincidences' are really His hand guiding us."

I shrugged, unsure whether to believe him. "Maybe," I said, "but you said that everything would work out right. You keep saying that, and everything keeps going wrong. How can everything work out now that Mr. Zaiden knows who I am and is probably going to kill us?" I glared at Luke, expecting to hear the same answer again.

"You know, I think you're forgetting that we have an enemy. The devil doesn't want us to win. He wants evil to win, but you know what?" Luke paused, waiting for my answer. I just shrugged. "God is stronger than the devil. He proved that by raising Jesus from the dead. The devil is already defeated. We have God on our side, and He will help us be victorious. Things may not always go according to our plan, but God has a greater plan that we can't see. He is in control. We just have to trust Him."

I let those words sink in. After a pause, I said, "I guess I never thought of it that way."

Luke nodded and opened his car door. He stepped out of the car, then turned back to face me. "You know, I said we have God on our side and that He'll help us. But I wonder if you personally have God on your side or if you're trying to fight evil with your own strength."

I glared at him. "So?" I asked defensively. "I know God exists, but He doesn't seem to really care."

"You've said that before, yet you seem to be questioning what you believe," Luke said. He walked around to my side of the truck and opened the door for me. He offered his hand to me and helped me step out of the truck.

We silently walked down the steps into his office. My mind raced. *I asked God for faith, but everything keeps going wrong. Why should I have faith?*

Luke pushed the metal desk off the trapdoor.

Luke has faith, and he has peace and hope. I want that, I thought.

"Luke," I said, after the desk quit scraping across the floor, "I asked God for faith the other day. I want the kind of faith you have, but I just ... I just can't seem to get it."

Luke smiled gently. "Faith is the assurance of things hoped for, the conviction of things not seen. You want to have faith? You need to take the risk of having faith in God," he said.

I rolled my eyes. "You make it sound so easy. I happen to know it's not," I replied.

"What do you mean?" Luke asked, leaning against the desk. He waited, an expectant look on his face.

I shrugged. "Let's just say there was an incident in my life where everyone told me I just needed to have faith in God— that God would see me through. It didn't ... it didn't work out. Nothing did from that point on," I said, staring down at my feet. I crossed my arms and leaned against the wall, hoping Luke would change the subject.

"So something went wrong in your life, and you felt like God let you down?" Luke asked, raising an eyebrow. I shrugged and nodded. Luke paused for a moment, his eyes closed. Finally, he looked back at me and said, "All of us will experience hard times. There's no doubt about that. Jesus never promised that He would make your life perfect here on earth. He promised peace for the hard times, and hope and strength. He also promised that after this life, those who believe in Him get to live in eternity with Him, where there will be no more pain or sorrow. You said that I make faith sound so easy, and the truth is, sometimes it is, and sometimes it isn't. But through it all, Christ is with us. He'll never leave you. He never has. It's up to you to let Him into your heart, because He's not forcing any of us to love Him." Luke paused and took a deep breath. "Well, what do you think?"

His question startled me. "What do you mean?" I asked.

"What do you think? Are you ready to have faith in God, or are you still doubting?" Luke asked, his eyes wide with anticipation.

I looked down at my feet again. I felt something inside me nudging me toward what Luke was saying. I had butterflies in my stomach, and my heart began pounding. *You need to make a choice. You asked for faith. Are you going to take it or leave it?*

I thought over the events of the day, the events ever since Luke and Sarah had showed up. It seemed like bad luck was following me, but following the bad luck was always something to help fix the problem. *Luke said God would work things out for good. Each time I thought everything was over, we found a new plan,* I thought. *But what about right now? An assassin is out to get you. You've been fired. There is a possibility of your entire mission failing.*

I looked up to find Luke smiling at me. "What do you say?"

I took a deep breath, trying to calm my fearful heart. "I want faith like yours. If God is the One who can give me that kind of confidence, then I want Him," I replied as confidently as I could.

Luke's small smile erupted into pure joy. "Hallelujah, amen!" he cried, jumping up and doing a fist pump. Grabbing my hand, he sank to his knees, and I followed him.

I prayed, asking God for faith, for the hope and peace He promised me. As I prayed, I felt the butterflies in my stomach turn into excitement, and tears began to roll down my cheeks.

Luke prayed afterward, and as he prayed, I felt calm. My fears about failing our mission melted away as Luke finished his prayer, "Lord, we trust You with this battle. Give us victory through Your mighty power! In Christ's name, we pray, amen."

I opened my eyes and looked at Luke. He looked as though he'd cried a few tears too, but his face was ecstatic. "Welcome to the family of God!" he cried, giving me a big hug.

CHAPTER 10

That night I stayed with Sarah in her hotel room, since we had all decided it would be too dangerous for me to go home. "Mr. Zaiden knows where you live because of the tracking bug," Sarah had said and then insisted that I stay with her. "We can get all your equipment from your house in the morning."

"And make sure there are no more tracking bugs," Luke put in.

"Right," I said, too tired to think of any other plan.

***

The next morning we headed to my apartment. Luke and I decided to disguise ourselves while Sarah pretended to be me.

Arriving at the apartment, we found a few police cars parked outside the building. "What's going on?" Sarah asked, looking worried. The three of us hurried inside to find out.

"Oh, Rebecca! I'm glad you're here," the apartment manager said. He walked up to Sarah, his eyes wide with excitement. "Someone broke into your apartment last night."

"What?" Sarah said, her eyes widening. A nearby officer asked Sarah to show him an ID, and after looking at my ID, which Sarah held, he began answering questions.

"Late last night," the officer explained, "your neighbors said they heard noises in your apartment. They assumed it was you at first, since you often come home late. However, after hearing a lot of scraping and banging, they got suspicious. One of your neighbors went to knock on your door and found the lock broken, so she called us."

"Did you catch the person who broke in?" Sarah asked urgently.

The officer shook his head. "We arrived as soon as possible, but the intruder was already gone. We've done a thorough investigation but haven't got much," he said.

"Have you found fingerprints or anything like that?" Sarah asked impatiently.

"We've been waiting to see your fingerprints, ma'am, so we know which ones aren't yours," the officer said. "Let me go get the fingerprint scanner."

"Okay," Sarah said, glancing at me.

"I need to step outside for a moment. This excitement is making me dizzy," I said, walking wobbly toward the door, hoping Sarah would catch on.

Sarah turned to face me, looking confused. I nodded toward the door with my head as discreetly as I could. Sarah's eyes widened with understanding and said, "Oh, let me get the door for you, honey." She hurried over and opened the door, helping me over to the bench to sit down.

"We're identical twins, but we don't have identical fingerprints," I whispered.

"What are we going to do about that? We can't switch outfits—there's not enough time," Sarah whispered.

I thought for a minute, then said, "Go to the car and grab my water bottle and purse from the trunk."

"Okay," she said and hurried to the car. She returned with

the requested items. "Here you go," she said, handing me the water.

"Thanks," I replied and took a sip as she placed the purse in my lap. Setting my water bottle next to my purse, I opened my purse and pulled out a sticker sheet Luke had given me. "This is Luke's fake fingerprint invention. It's never been tested before," I warned, placing my thumb on one of the stickers.

"This is the perfect time to test it then," Sarah said.

"Okay, give me your thumb," I said as I peeled the sticker off the page, the sticker still on my thumb. I pressed the sticker onto Sarah's thumb and then slowly pulled it off. Her thumb now had my fingerprint on it. "Let's see how this works," I said, smiling at her. She patted me on the back and then stood up and reentered the building. *Lord, please let that sticker work. Otherwise we're in trouble*, I prayed quickly, then stood up and went back into the building.

"Oh, she's fine," I heard Sarah say to the officer. "She's just shook up by the excitement."

The officer glanced up at me, raising an eyebrow. I faked a weak smile. He shrugged and continued with his investigation. He held out a metal box with a large hole in the side. "Place your thumb in here please," he said, and Sarah obeyed. The officer pressed a button on the top of the box, and a few seconds later said, "Thank you. You can remove your thumb now."

Sarah removed her thumb. "Is there anything else you need me to do?" she asked.

"We need you to tell us if anything was stolen last night. We've left your apartment as closely as we could to how we found it," the officer said, leading us up the stairs.

"I'll do my best, sir," Sarah said, glancing at me.

We spent an hour going through my apartment to see

what was stolen. All my files on completed cases were gone. My laptop and Taser were gone. Everything else was still there.

"We'll try to find the burglar as soon as possible," the officer said as we walked back downstairs.

"Thank you. Is it all right for me to leave now? I need to get to work," Sarah said.

"Yes. You're free to go, but please leave your number with us so we can get ahold of you at any time," the officer said, handing her a pad of paper and a pencil. She wrote down her number, and we left the building.

"Well, that was ... awesome," Luke said sarcastically as he got into his car.

"Mm-hmm," Sarah agreed. We got in and buckled up as Luke started the car.

"What do we do now?" I asked.

"I'm not sure," Luke replied, driving back to his office. "I'm pretty sure we know who broke in, though."

"Mr. Zaiden?" Sarah said, raising her eyebrows.

"Most likely, although he could have sent Lisa instead," I suggested. "If they do find fingerprints, then it probably means Lisa broke in, not Mr. Zaiden. He's too experienced to make a rookie mistake like that."

"Unless he was trying to scare you," Luke put in.

I shrugged. *He does like to scare people into obeying him*, I thought.

That evening we were at Luke's office, getting our gear together. "Do you think our plan will actually work?" Sarah asked, pulling out gadgets from a box.

"It'd better," I muttered.

"Totally! You just need a little confidence. We can do this," Luke said, striking a superhero pose.

"But it's three of us versus all Mr. Zaiden's guards," I said, putting my hands on my hips. "It's a long shot."

Luke waved his hand. "Don't forget, we have God on our side. We've just got to go for it!"

Sarah placed the box back on the shelf. "So we have to sneak past the guards tonight, right? Then Luke and I create a distraction while you get to the basement to get the evidence against Mr. Zaiden," Sarah said, pointing at me.

"Yes. After I get the info, we all make a run for it back to the car and take the information straight to the FBI," I finished.

Sarah took a deep breath and smiled. "Okay, I think we can do this," she said, sounding more confident than she looked.

"Oh, dear," Luke said. He held a thin computer screen attached to an armband. "We need new batteries," he said, tapping on the screen. "It's dead."

"It's not rechargeable?" Sarah asked, taking it from him.

"No. Matthew and I didn't think of that feature when we made it," Luke said, sounding a little embarrassed.

"Can I see that?" I asked. Sarah handed it to me, and I looked it over. *The technology on this thing is amazing*, I thought. Luke had shown me how it worked a few days ago. It was an ultrathin computer with extra high-speed Internet, the fastest I'd ever seen. It had tons of memory storage, especially for such a small device, and a voice command option. There were three of these computers, and they linked to each other on their own frequency, allowing communication, GPS tracking, and, I assumed, much more.

"There's one for each of us. This one is just out of batteries," Luke said.

We looked for batteries on the shelves and desk but couldn't find any.

"I can go to the store and buy some more," Sarah offered.

I shook my head no. "That's a bad idea."

"Why?" she asked.

"Because we're identical twins. We don't want Mr. Zaiden to find you and think you're me," I said, wondering why she hadn't thought of this.

Luke thought for a moment. "Well, she could just wear one of your wigs," he suggested.

"But Mr. Zaiden has seen me wear both of my wigs," I argued.

"Look, I'll be fine. I'll take different routes there and back. Now, do we need anything else?" she asked.

"Doughnuts and pizza," Luke replied quickly. I raised an eyebrow. "For energy, of course," he said as though the answer were totally obvious.

I rolled my eyes. "If we think of anything important that we need, we'll text you. But I'm serious. You need to be super careful."

"Okay. See you in a jiffy," Sarah said with a wave. She turned and hurried out the hatch.

"Are you sure she should go by herself?" I asked Luke worriedly.

"We have work to do here. I'm sure Sarah will be fine," he replied confidently, though his frequent glances at the hatch made me think otherwise.

Luke and I reviewed our plan several times as we finished getting the equipment ready. The more we reviewed our plan, the more excited I got. "This might just work," I said, sitting down after we'd finished.

"Just might? Dude, our plan is awesome. I am so ready for

this!" Luke cried, pumping his fist. He plopped down in the chair next to me, a mysterious grin spreading across his face. "We just have to wait till nightfall."

"I'm glad you have so much energy," I said, laughing.

Luke just shrugged. "Yeah, but I'm in need of a refill. When is Sarah going to get back? I'm starving."

I stopped laughing. "She has been gone a little longer than I expected," I said, crossing my arms.

"She wore her watch today, right?" Luke asked as he pulled his chair over to the computer.

"Yes," I said, following him.

Luke pulled up her watch's information on the screen. "Let me check her tracker," he said, clicking a few buttons. A map of the city pulled up with a flashing green light moving around on the screen.

"She's not headed our way," I said, watching the light move away from the store.

Luke's voice filled with concern. "She's not on foot. Her tracker is moving too fast for her to even be running."

"And she didn't take your car," I said, panic rising in me. "What if—"

"No what-ifs," Luke interrupted. "One of us needs to go find out what's up."

"I'll go," I said, grabbing my watch. I headed for the hatch.

Luke followed behind me. "Maybe I should go instead," he said.

I turned around and shook my head. "You stay here and monitor what's going on. I'll stay in contact with you." Before Luke could argue any more, I climbed the ladder, opened the hatch, and hurried out of the basement. *I knew she shouldn't have gone to the store*, I thought.

Twenty minutes later, I stood behind a tree just outside Mr. Zaiden's property. I sent a quick message to Luke on my watch. "Is Sarah here?"

He replied seconds later. "Yes. Inside building."

I peeked out from around the tree to see who was on guard. I noticed Mr. Zaiden had finished installing the new security system in the short time I'd been gone. *Mr. Zaiden must really not want me getting back in*, I thought, scanning the area. Just outside the gate stood Jerry, one of the newer security guards.

I sent Luke another message. "Security upgraded. No chance breaking in, but I have a plan."

"What's your idea?" he answered.

I quickly typed back, "I might be able to bribe Jerry into helping us."

Luke's response came quickly. "Sounds risky."

I rolled my eyes. "Going for it," I typed quickly and sent the message.

God, please let this work, I prayed. Standing up straight and putting on a confident face, I walked out from behind the tree into Jerry's view, being careful to stay in the shadows so the cameras didn't pick me up.

"Who's there?" Jerry cried, pulling out his gun. "Put your hands in the air."

"They're in the air," I replied sarcastically, pulling my hands up to my shoulders. "But you'd better put the gun down and get over here."

Jerry stepped toward me. "Who are you? Don't you know we're closed?"

I forced a laugh and shook my head. "Of course I do, Jerry."

He took a step back. "How do you know my name?" he asked, bracing himself.

"You should know mine," I replied, grinning slyly.

Jerry cocked his head to the side, confused. Slowly he stepped forward. "Mariah?" he asked, sounding shocked. "But how did you ..."

Seeing he was close enough, I made my move. I kicked his gun out of his hand and pulled him into the shadows. Grabbing the Taser from my belt, I pushed him up to the tree and whispered, "Don't make any wrong moves, or I'll shoot."

Jerry's breathing was shaky. "How did you escape?" he asked nervously. "I saw Zaiden take you inside, all handcuffed and stuff."

"Oh you did, did you?" I asked. "Well, I'll have you know that I have a double."

"Really?" Jerry cried, his eyes widening.

"Oh, yes, and it's all a part of the plan. My double is still inside—on purpose, you see. Mr. Zaiden won't be around much longer," I said, faking total confidence.

Jerry seemed to be buying the act. "What ... what are you gonna do?" he asked nervously.

"Take his operation down, along with him and all his allies. Of course, I could spare you, on one condition," I said, trying to sound mysterious.

"How do I know you're not lying?" Jerry asked, sounding suspicious.

I pressed my Taser into his back and wrapped an arm around his neck as fast as I could. "Mr. Zaiden may be an expert assassin, but I'm better," I threatened.

"Okay, okay, okay! I'll help you!" Jerry cried, obviously frightened.

"Good," I said, releasing his neck. "Tomorrow evening at

eleven thirty, I'll come and visit you. You'll let me into the property, and no security systems will go off. Understand?" I pressed my Taser into his back again.

"Understood," he replied shakily.

I took a step back. "And you'd better not rat on us, or you won't get any share," I said.

I got the response I hoped for. "Share of what?" Jerry asked, turning around.

"The money, of course. Don't you know Mr. Zaiden is a billionaire?" I said, emphasizing the last word.

"He is?" Jerry exclaimed. I shushed him.

"Just remember the deal," I said, backing away. "And remember my warning." Once I felt I was far enough away to be safe, I turned around and took off for Luke's office.

⌐

"Good news and bad news," I cried, jumping into the computer room and rolling onto the floor. It was faster than climbing down the ladder.

Luke offered me a hand up. He looked rather annoyed. "I can't believe you," he said, shaking his head. "One risk after another."

"I'm just following in your footsteps. Now, do you want to hear my news or not?" I said, putting my hands on my hips.

"Sure. Start with the good news," Luke said, crossing his arms.

"Good news is, Jerry is gonna let us in tomorrow night at eleven thirty. We'll get through the outside security easy as pie," I said with a nod of satisfaction.

Luke smiled. "That's one task made easier. But what's the bad news?" He raised an eyebrow expectantly.

I took a deep breath. "Jerry confirmed that Sarah was kidnapped by Mr. Zaiden," I said, and panic started rising inside me. "He said that Mr. Zaiden's men thought she was me."

Luke's face grew serious, and he looked worried.

"What are we going to do?" I cried, sinking to the floor. "What if they hurt her or kill her? It'll be all my fault because they thought she was me. What are we going to do?" I tried to hold back my tears, but they ended up spilling out anyway. "And our plan! We needed Sarah to help us. Now it's just bound to go wrong, and ... and ... we need to rescue Sarah, but I don't know ..." *We were finally sisters again after all this time, and now ... now I may never see her again,* I worried inwardly.

Luke sat down beside me and patted me on the back. "Calm down," he replied softly. The worry he'd shown before was gone. "We'll just adjust our plan."

"Adjust our plan?" I cried, frustrated. "And how do we do that? Our original plan has been adjusted a thousand different times. Every time something goes wrong, you say, 'Adjust the plan,' and every time we do, something else goes wrong."

"Arguing won't help us," Luke said, his voice agitated. "We have to pull our plan together by tomorrow night. Now quit panicking, and let's think of a plan." Luke closed his eyes and took a deep breath. "Sorry for yelling at you."

"No, you're right. We need to calm down and think," I replied. "I just ... I don't know what to do." I shook my head sadly, wondering whether I would ever see Sarah again.

Luke smiled at me. "Trust in the Lord with all your heart and do not lean on your own understanding. In all your ways acknowledge Him, and He will make your paths straight."

"Maybe we should pray first, then think," I said quietly.

"You just read my mind," Luke said with a grin. He grabbed my hand and then began praying. "Lord, our plans keep getting messed up. It seems like the bad guys might win this time, but we know You are stronger than our enemies. We ask for Your guidance as we strategize. Give us victory for Your name and Your glory. And please keep Sarah safe. Protect all of us. In Christ's name, we pray, amen."

"Amen," I echoed, wiping the tears off my face. I opened my eyes to see Luke's face full of excitement.

He grinned at me as he stood. "I think I have an idea."

CHAPTER 11

"What time is it?" I asked, walking out of the science lab.

"Ten forty-seven," Luke replied as he stuck an earpiece into his left ear. "Are you geared up?"

"Yup," I said, grabbing my armband computer from off the desk. We were both dressed completely in black with bulletproof leather jackets. We didn't have to worry about disguising our gadgets this time. We both had tool belts full of gadgets—earpieces, computers, watches, Tasers, guns, grenades—pretty much everything we could possibly carry on ourselves.

Luke pulled on his black gloves, then smiled at me. "I think I'm ready."

I took a deep breath and told myself to be confident. "You're ready for your part of the plan?" I asked.

"Yes," Luke replied seriously. "I go after Sarah, and you go after the information about Zaiden."

I nodded, going over the details of my half of the plan in my mind. It was risky, but we had no other choice. "Are you sure your friends will come?" I asked, trying not to sound nervous.

"Positive." Luke checked his watch again. "Okay, ten minutes till we leave."

"Then it's time to pray," I replied.

Luke pulled the car to a stop a block away from Mr. Zaiden's office. "You ready for this?" he asked, grinning excitedly.

"Oh, yeah!" I replied, opening my car door. The thrill of the mission was getting to both of us, and I was reminded why I loved being an agent so much. *Too bad this will be the last one I do in a while,* I thought as we made our way down the street. I shook that thought from my head and turned my thoughts to the mission. This was too important for me to be distracted by what would happen later.

Staying in the shadows, Luke led the way to the front gate. Jerry stood just outside, looking around nervously. Luke nodded, and our plan went into action.

As quickly and quietly as possible, I made my way over to Jerry. I tapped his shoulder and then covered his mouth so he wouldn't scream. "It's Mariah," I whispered in his ear. "Are the cameras ready?"

Jerry nodded. "I just have to flip the switch in the control room," he whispered, nodding toward the shed behind us.

"Lead the way," I replied and followed him. After he flipped the switch, we went back over to the gate, and I signaled for Luke.

"Don't alert Zaiden, or else you get no share," I warned, and Luke and I hurried through the gate.

Reaching the door of the building, we saw who was on guard inside. "It's Lisa," I whispered.

"Can we sneak past her?" Luke asked as he began unlocking the door using his invention.

I shrugged. "I don't know," I whispered.

We heard the door click. "We're in," Luke said. "Get ready." He held up three fingers. I grabbed my Taser. He put one finger down. I got ready to charge. He put another finger down. With that he shoved the door open, and I took off.

"What's going on here?" Lisa cried, reaching for her radio. I shot my Taser before she could radio for help. She fell to the floor, shaking.

"You go downstairs. I'll go up," I said and took off. I headed straight to the computer control room. As I entered the third floor, I saw another guard next to the control room's door. He had his phone out and didn't seem to notice my presence. I slowly walked toward him. I pointed my Taser, ready to fire, when he looked up.

"What are you doing out of the basement?" he asked, but that was as far as he got.

I put my Taser away and entered the pass code for the control room. I was surprised to find it was still the same. "I'm in," I whispered into my earpiece. Then I pushed the door open and stepped inside.

"Why, hello, Rebecca. I've been expecting you," Mr. Zaiden said, an evil grin spread across his face. He stood on the other side of the desk in the middle of the room next to the main computer, the one I wanted to use.

"Well, that's so sweet of you," I said sarcastically. Seeing Mr. Zaiden in the control room, I realized my half of the plan wasn't going to work. I couldn't get the necessary information with him standing right there. "Zaiden's here," I muttered into my earpiece, hoping to alert Luke.

"I heard my guard ask how you got out of the basement. I could ask the same thing, but I already know the answer," Mr. Zaiden said.

"Oh you do?" I said, stepping toward him.

"Of course. You seemed like yourself for a while until I noticed the stance, the voice, and the eyes."

"What about those things?" I asked, hoping Mr. Zaiden would be distracted long enough for me to form a plan.

"Yes. The stance and the voice were too gentle, and the eyes, well, they were too expressive. This was not the acting job I have come to expect from you. No, I did my research and found out that you have an identical twin. A very identical twin," Mr. Zaiden said, sounding pleased with himself.

"Good for you," I replied.

"And now you know why I was expecting you," he said, nodding.

"What?" I asked, caught off guard.

"Of course. Twins always copy each other," he said. Without warning he jumped in my direction and threw an object at me. I dodged it, and it hit the wall, causing a small explosion. I instinctively rolled onto the floor and away from the blast. I hopped up, only to have Mr. Zaiden push me down. He stood over me and pointed a gun at my face.

"You've got two options," he said, but I rolled to the left and pushed on his leg, knocking him over. I slid out of the way and tried to run, but then I felt an arm wrap around my neck.

"You've got two options," Mr. Zaiden said again.

"You already said that," I choked out. I regretted that comment as he tightened his headlock.

"You run the EMP for me, or you can say goodbye to the world," he said. I opened my mouth to speak, but he continued, "And your twin will die with you. It's your choice."

"She has nothing to do with this," I whispered.

"Oh, yes, she does. We both know she has too much information. Now make up your mind." Mr. Zaiden's grip loosened slightly.

I took a deep breath and prayed, *Lord, what do I do? Help me!*

Then an idea struck me—the self-destruct. The building had a self-destruct code. *If only I could get over to the main computer ...*

I shoved my elbow into Mr. Zaiden's ribs. He let go of my neck, and I bolted forward. I was headed away from Mr. Zaiden but also the main computer. I ran around to the other side of the desk, hoping to beat Mr. Zaiden to the computer.

"Stop!" Mr. Zaiden cried.

I glanced over at him, and he picked up his gun. I ducked behind the desk just before he shot. The bullet hit the wall.

"You had the makings of a perfect assassin, one to take my place, and you ruined your chance," Mr. Zaiden said. I began crawling toward the main computer. "I gave you multiple opportunities for greatness, but instead of showing gratitude, you betrayed me."

I reached the corner of the desk. Grabbing my gun, I shot at the door. I heard footsteps headed toward the door. Seizing the opportunity, I bolted over to the computer and turned it on. I entered the password. Just as the computer unlocked, a bullet whizzed past my shoulder. I ducked behind the desk again.

"Stay away from my computer!" Mr. Zaiden shouted, and I heard him walk in my direction.

One, two, three, four. I counted his steps. *Five, six ... now!* I jumped from my hiding spot and onto Mr. Zaiden, pushing the gun out of his hand.

"Give that back!" he cried, tripping me. I grabbed the gun as I fell. He tried to wrestle it out of my hand, but I kicked him in the stomach and sent him flying backward.

I darted for the door, opened it, and threw both his gun and mine down the hall. I turned around to see Mr. Zaiden jumping toward me. I ran and ducked, letting him sail over me, and then charged back over to the computer.

I pulled up the power files and entered the access code. After it loaded, I began searching for the self-destruction code. Before I got that far, Mr. Zaiden charged and pushed me onto the floor. He reached to turn the computer off, but I jumped up and shoved him out of the way. I pulled up the file labeled "SD code."

"Here it is!" I muttered, reading the code. "SDCODE100."

I felt my leg being pulled and fell face-first onto the floor. I hopped back up and pushed Mr. Zaiden away from the computer.

He swung a fist at me. I blocked it. We started a fist fight, but I could tell I wasn't a very good match for Mr. Zaiden. He was much stronger than I.

One blow hit the side of my face, knocking my earpiece out.

Outsmart him then, I told myself. With the next big swing he took, I darted to the left, and his fist hit air. His momentum pulled him into the wall. I ran back to the computer.

Typing as fast as possible, I entered, "S-D-C-O-D-E-1-0-0." Just before I hit "enter," he pushed me to the ground.

Mr. Zaiden stood over me, this time with a knife in his hand. He smiled at me, his eyes emotionless. I was unable to move ... time seemed to stand still.

"Adios," he said and pulled his hand back.

I'm gonna die! I thought, panicking.

Suddenly Mr. Zaiden cried out in pain as his arm was pulled backward.

"Sarah!" I cried.

She tried to wrestle the knife from Mr. Zaiden.

I pulled myself out from under him and stood up. Now was my chance. I took my place at the computer and hit "enter."

"Please confirm your password" flashed onto the screen. I sighed in frustration and reentered the password.

"Rebecca, look out!" Sarah cried. I jumped to the side, and Mr. Zaiden's knife barely missed me. The knife landed on the keyboard, hitting the "enter" button.

"Self-destruction commencing," the computer's robotic voice said. "Ninety seconds remaining."

A large, metal box fell out of the ceiling and slammed down on the computer. "No!" Mr. Zaiden cried, trying to move the box.

"Eighty-nine seconds," the voice said from the speakers.

"We need to get out of here. This building is going to explode!" I cried, ushering Sarah toward the door.

"No! All my plans ... my research!" Mr. Zaiden cried, pulling at the box in vain.

"If you want to live, you'd better leave now," I said and dashed out the door behind Sarah.

Sarah ran straight for the stairs. "Is he following us?" she puffed.

"I don't know," I replied, glancing over my shoulder. The guard I had knocked out was now conscious and stood up shakily.

"Eighty-six seconds," the speaker boomed.

"Eighty-six what?" the guard said groggily.

"The building is going to explode! Get out of here!" Mr. Zaiden's deep voice yelled at the guard. For the first time, his voice had a slight hint of fear.

Sarah led the way down the stairs, flight after flight.

"Seventy-five seconds."

I heard a gunshot behind me. "Stop those girls!" Mr. Zaiden cried.

"Jump!" I said as we reached the last flight. We jumped to the bottom of the stairs and pushed at the door. "It's locked!" I cried.

"Great," Sarah said, looking panicked.

"Seventy seconds," the speaker boomed just as a guard ran up from the basement.

"What is going on?" he asked, pulling his gun off his belt.

"The building is going to blow up," Sarah and I said in unison.

I nodded and continued, "We need to get out of here before we blow up with it. Can you unlock this door?"

The guard, looking confused, nodded and pulled his key card out of his pocket. He unlocked the door and pushed it open.

"Stop right there!" Mr. Zaiden yelled from behind us. I turned around to see him and his guard with their guns pointed at us. "I will not let you destroy all my work. You will come back and turn off the self-destruct."

"I can't," I cried. "There is no override password, unless you made one." I didn't know whether to hope he knew the password or to hope he didn't have one. The look on his face told me he didn't have one. "We need to get out of here before we all are destroyed in the explosion."

Everyone was silent. Mr. Zaiden glared at me as the overhead speakers continued their countdown. "Sixty seconds."

"Guards, take that one," Mr. Zaiden said, pointing to Sarah, "to the edge of the property and wait for me."

"Yes, sir," the guards said. They grabbed Sarah's arms and pulled her out the door.

Mr. Zaiden grabbed my arm and pushed me out the door too, but then we started walking in the other direction. "What are we doing?" I asked.

"We're going to save my work," Mr. Zaiden replied angrily.

"The EMP?" I watched Mr. Zaiden's face, hoping for an answer, but he didn't give it.

We reached the hangar just as the speakers announced, "Twenty seconds."

I pulled out of Mr. Zaiden's grasp and turned to face him, blocking the door to the hangar. "Listen to me. We have less than twenty seconds to get away. If you try to save your research, you won't get away from the explosion in time."

Mr. Zaiden stood there, his jaw tense. Finally he grunted, his face became expressionless, and he said, "Fine. If that's how it's going to be."

I hit the ground just before he shot. Before he could shoot again, I kicked the hangar door open and pulled myself inside, slamming the door shut. I stood up as I heard his footsteps running away.

"Ten seconds," the speaker blared, louder than before. I pulled the door open and took off as fast as I possibly could toward the back of the property.

"Nine seconds."

I saw a large scrap piece of metal lying on the ground not too far from me. *I hope that will protect me from the blast*, I thought as I charged for it.

"Eight seconds ... seven seconds ... six seconds ..."

I reached the metal and picked it up, dragging it farther away from the property.

"Five seconds ... four seconds ... three seconds ..."

I crouched down behind the metal piece, plugged my ears, and prayed for protection.

"Two seconds ..."

Wait a second. Where is Luke? I thought, realizing I hadn't seen him since we sneaked into the building.

"One second."

I had no more time to think. A deafening "BOOM" sounded behind me. I felt the blast pushing me over. I heard several more explosions, glass breaking, and the sound of metal and concrete hitting the ground. Eventually the noise died down, and all I could hear was the sound of flames flickering.

I pushed the scrap metal off my back and sat up slowly. My head and ears were pounding, but I was alive. "Thank You, Lord!" I breathed. I sat still, breathing slowly as I tried to calm down. I looked at the pile of metal and concrete lying not far from me. The little bit of building that was flammable was burning, but I knew the fire would quickly die out.

I heard sirens in the distance, growing louder. *Oh, good. The police are coming,* I thought, and that's when I remembered. "Where's Luke?" I cried, standing up. I felt a little lightheaded as I stood, but I shook off the feeling. I looked at my watch and my armband computer, but they were both busted, so I couldn't try to call him. I hurried as best as I could over to the other side of the property, hoping to find Luke with everyone else.

I got there just as the police pulled up. I made my way over to Sarah, who sat by the guardhouse, hugging her knees. "You okay?" I asked, sitting next to her.

"I hope so," she replied shakily. "I've never been on the site of an explosion before."

I nodded. "This was pretty massive."

"Don't tell me you've been on the site of explosions before," Sarah cried.

I smiled. "Okay, I won't," I said, taking a deep breath. I looked around. The medical team was attending to Mr. Zaiden. He looked like he had a few bad burns.

Another medic walked up to us. "Were you on-site when the building exploded?" he asked. We nodded. "All right. I need to make sure you don't have any injuries, although you'll probably still need to come to the hospital anyways just to be sure." He asked a few questions, then checked our heart rates and our eyes and ears. After he was sure we hadn't broken any bones or been burned, he reminded us to get a checkup again.

"I'm going to keep an eye on you," he said, pointing to me. "You may have a slight concussion."

The medic walked away, and an officer headed our way. Before he got there, I asked Sarah, "Where's Luke?"

Sarah's eyes grew wide and fearful. "I don't know! I haven't seen him since he rescued me from the basement."

Where would he have been the whole time? I wondered.

"Before I went to help you, he said something about getting information, and then he asked me to go help you. After that, he ran off," Sarah explained.

I turned to the officer who'd just walked up. "Sir, we have another friend who was here, and he's not with our group right now," I said, fearing the worst.

"Was he on the site before the explosion?" the officer asked.

I nodded, feeling dizzy again. "I don't know where he is."

"Don't worry, ma'am. We'll get some guys out there to find him," the officer said. "Do you think he was still in the building when it exploded?"

"We don't know," Sarah replied.

The officer radioed to another officer and told him about Luke. The officer asked a few more questions about where we'd last seen him, what he looked like, and such. I began to feel queasy and lightheaded.

What if he didn't make it out? I thought worriedly. And then everything went black.

I opened my eyes and blinked several times, trying to clear my vision. I was in a hospital room, and I had a terrible headache.

A nurse walked into the room and smiled at me. "Good morning, honey!" she said cheerfully. For a second I tried to figure out why I was in the hospital, and then I remembered the explosion.

"I'm guessing I had a concussion, huh?" I mumbled.

"What, honey?" the nurse asked.

I cleared my throat and tried again. "Did I have a concussion?"

The nurse nodded, still smiling. "Uh-huh. It wasn't too bad, though, considering the predicament you were in."

"I guess that's true." I glanced around. "Is my sister here?"

"Your sister? You mean, the identical one?" the nurse asked. I nodded. "Oh, yes. Well, she *was* here, but the police needed to continue the investigation. She's at the police station right now."

I closed my eyes, ready to fall asleep so my headache would leave, when I remembered Luke. "Did they find Luke?" I asked, feeling alarmed. I opened my eyes and tried to sit up, but I couldn't.

"Now, now, now. Calm down, honey. You just need to rest," the nurse said, patting my arm.

"But this is important! Did they find my friend? Is he okay?" I asked, feeling ready to scream or cry or both, although I didn't feel like I had energy to do either.

"Shh, it's okay. He'll be okay too. Now you go ahead and rest," the nurse said in a soothing voice. I needed more answers, but I was too tired to talk anymore, and I drifted off to sleep.

☞

I awoke later to my worried sister's voice next to me.

"But that's not fair!" Sarah was saying. She sounded like she was crying.

A deep voice replied, "Sarah, you know it is, but I'll see what I can do to get the program running." The voice seemed vaguely familiar, but I couldn't place it.

I opened my eyes and turned to see whom she was talking with. The man was tall with broad shoulders. He had dark hair with a little bit of gray sprinkled through it. He looked to be in his late thirties or early forties. He had an angular jaw, bright-blue eyes, and a peaceful face. He somehow looked familiar.

"Who is that?" I wondered, not realizing I'd said it aloud.

Sarah turned to face me excitedly. "Rebecca! You're awake!" She stood up and hugged me. I smiled at her, then nodded toward the doorway with a raised eyebrow. The man had stepped out of the room after Sarah hugged me.

"Oh, that's my boss," Sarah explained.

Sarah looked upset again, so I changed the subject. "Is Luke okay?"

"Yes, thankfully," she replied, her voice full of relief.

"What happened?" I asked.

"He went to find the documents we needed to implicate Mr. Zaiden," Sarah explained. "He was in the basement when the countdown began. He'd just opened one of the file cabinet doors and gotten the papers out. He didn't have enough time to get out of there, so he did the next best thing—he hid in the file cabinet."

"The cabinets weren't destroyed?" I asked, surprised.

"Nope. Apparently the self-destruct wasn't installed in the basement, so it didn't blow up. It stayed relatively intact despite the rest of the building falling on top of it," Sarah said. "Once the fire crew began looking through the rubble, they found Luke in the file cabinet. He was a little banged up, and the shock wave knocked him out, but he's doing better now. The doctor's going to let him leave the hospital the same time as you."

*

A few hours later Sarah, Luke, and I made our way out of the hospital. I couldn't keep the smile off my face. We were all safe, and the mission had been accomplished.

Luke was his usual, animated self. "Man, I can't wait to eat lunch," he said as we walked out the door. "I'm starving. Twenty-four hours with no food does not sit well with me."

I smiled at him. "I have to admit I'm rather hungry, too."

As we walked into the parking lot, two police officers came our way, looking grim. "Rebecca Sanders?" the first one said, waiting for one of us girls to reply.

"That's me," I replied hesitantly.

The two policemen turned to me, the second one pulling handcuffs off his belt. "Rebecca Sanders," the first said, "you are under arrest."

CHAPTER 12

I sat in a jail cell, trying not to cry. The police told me the FBI had gone through the files salvaged from the explosion. With Mr. Zaiden's careful record keeping, there was no denying my involvement as a master assassin's assistant. I didn't even try to deny it either. I knew it would do me no good, and I would end up with a greater jail sentence if I lied, so I admitted to everything. I answered every question truthfully and gave them the details of the explosion. It felt good to know I didn't have to hide anymore. Everything was now known, and Mr. Zaiden would be behind bars for the rest of his life. But I would be behind bars for quite some time as well.

I leaned against the wall, praying as best I could. *God, please let them have mercy on me. I don't want to spend forever in jail.* I took a deep breath and blinked hard so I wouldn't cry and tried to think of something else.

I thought over the files Mr. Zaiden had that I'd never seen before. *I wonder what those were all about,* I thought. *Let's see, there were several files—"PBPC," "Assignments," "$$$," "Assassin," and "America." What does America have to do with all this?* I thought back over the conversations I'd had with Mr. Zaiden about his plans and the phone call I'd overheard. *There was more to this than I knew,* I thought. Then it struck me—the phone call.

"He wasn't working alone," I muttered. I stood up and began pacing. I knew I needed to tell someone about this fact I'd overlooked.

I waved to the police officer on duty. "Excuse me!" I called, hoping she would listen to me.

"What do you want?" she asked with a huff.

"I need to talk to someone. It's urgent!" I said, using all my acting skills to be convincing.

"Let me guess—you want to talk to your lawyer," she said, sounding bored. She sat still, not moving.

"No. I need to talk to the FBI or Luke or Sarah. Someone involved with the Zaiden case!" I cried, feeling desperate.

The officer shrugged. "I'll talk to the sergeant," she replied, then hit a button on the intercom.

Please let them believe me, I prayed, waiting for her to finish her conversation.

Moments later the guard called back. "Okay, you're in luck. The sergeant says an agent is already here to see you." She stood up and made her way over to my jail cell. "Come with me, and you can talk to him on the other side of the glass," she said, unlocking the door.

We walked down the long hall past all the jail cells and entered through a metal door into a room with a window on the far side, facing another room. The officer motioned for me to sit in the chair next to the window, then radioed the sergeant. Seconds later the sergeant stepped into the opposite room, followed by a tall man with dark hair and blue eyes.

Sarah's boss? I thought, shocked.

Sarah's boss took his seat across from me, and the sergeant took up his position by the door to the other room. "How do you do?" the man asked, smiling.

"Fine," I said, unsure why this man was here. "May I ask who you are?"

He laughed and shook his head. "I'm sorry. I forgot that you don't really know me. It's your sister who knows me. Anyways, my name is John."

"John?" I asked, waiting for a last name.

"I go by John Truth," he said. I raised an eyebrow, so he continued, "You see, my real last name is extremely long, so I go by the nickname I received when I took over my father's position in Truth Squad. Most people call me Mr. Truth."

"Interesting," I replied. "So why are you here?"

"Yes, well, I wanted to let you know that we appreciate your help in solving this case, and we are trying to work out a deal with the FBI," he said quickly.

"Hold on. Who is 'we,' and what do you have to do with solving the case? And are you connected to the FBI?" I asked suspiciously.

"To answer the last question, yes, I am connected to the FBI, although I'm not an FBI agent," he said.

"Do you have a badge or something? I have really important information I need to get to the FBI," I said impatiently. "If you're not actually FBI, then I'm wasting my time, so—"

"Okay, okay, here's the badge," Mr. Truth said, pulling a badge from his coat pocket. It read "Truth Squad" across the top, and next to the name "John Truth" it read, "President of Truth Squad and Truth Academy."

"You're president of Truth Academy?" I asked.

"Yup," he replied, smiling. "If I'm recalling correctly, you used to be a student there."

I shrugged and turned my attention back to the problem at hand. "This doesn't prove to me that you're with the FBI."

Just then the sergeant opened the door to the room, and

in walked a man in a navy blue suit, white shirt, and tie. He wore an American flag pin on his lapel.

"Sorry I'm late," the man said, sitting down next to Mr. Truth. "The proposal did go through. That's what took me so long."

"Thank you, sir," Mr. Truth replied.

The agent introduced himself as Mr. Brandon and showed me his badge. I took a deep breath. *Okay, I guess I'll just have to trust them,* I thought and quickly launched into the details regarding Mr. Zaiden's boss and larger plan. I told them about the files, Mr. Zaiden's phone call, and Max.

Mr. Brandon listened intently the whole time, taking notes as I talked. When I finished, he nodded and said, "This answers a lot of questions regarding several confusing documents that were salvaged."

"But it also brings up many more questions," Mr. Truth countered.

"Like who is Max and what was really going on?" the agent said.

"It's too bad the computer system was destroyed," I said, crossing my arms. "If we got the codes from Mr. Zaiden, we would be able to have access to the real plans."

"But why wouldn't Zaiden tell you the whole plan if he insisted you were his top agent?" Mr. Truth asked.

I shrugged. "Probably because I didn't pass his test. You don't just trust people in this ... I mean, his business."

The FBI agent nodded and stood. "Well, I need to get this information to my team. We may be able to find more clues in the documents we salvaged. Thank you for your help, Ms. Sanders," he said, then walked out.

"Time's up," the officer behind me said. She walked up and grabbed my arm.

"We'll keep in touch," Mr. Truth said. He stood, smiled, and walked out the door on his side.

***

I awoke early the next morning, feeling stiff and uncomfortable. The bed in my jail cell was too hard compared to my own, but I tried to ignore that thought. *You'll have to be here a while. Might as well get used to it*, I told myself. I sat up in bed and leaned against the wall.

The trial for the case on Mr. Zaiden would be in two days. After his trial was over, I would have to go through the sentencing process. I had one small hope, and that was that I pleaded guilty. *Hopefully that, along with my help to the FBI, will get me a little grace and a shorter sentence*, I thought.

"Hey, you." I jumped at the voice of the officer standing outside my cell door. "Come with me. There's someone here to talk to you." She unlocked my door and opened it.

I stood up and followed her back to the room with the glass window. On the other side sat Mr. Truth and Sarah. Sarah's grin covered her whole face, and she practically bounced in her seat with excitement. *This must be good*, I thought as I took my seat across from them.

"Good morning," Mr. Truth said, sounding very businesslike. "I hope this meeting wasn't too early for you."

I shook my head no. "I figured not," Sarah said, grinning. She glanced impatiently at Mr. Truth.

He nodded. "Rebecca, we at Truth Squad have a proposition to make," he began. I nodded for him to continue. "Well, first I'd better explain what Truth Squad is."

"Seriously?" Sarah cried impatiently.

I shrugged. "Okay, that's probably a good idea, considering I've only heard of Truth Academy."

Mr. Truth nodded. "Truth Squad is a private Christian organization that partners with the FBI and the CIA. We take on important cases nationally and internationally that don't make the government's top priority list due to lack of resources. The goal of Truth Squad is really to defend the truth throughout the world—thus the name."

"Sounds good," I replied. I smiled as Sarah sighed impatiently and motioned for him to hurry up.

"All right, now for the proposition," Mr. Truth continued. "We've been working with the FBI and the government for some time to start a parole program at Truth Squad, a program where selected persons with jail sentences, with the government's permission, may come and serve out their time in Truth Squad under our supervision and direction. The government would determine the amount of time a person is on parole, and the parolee's time would be spent on our campus doing community service. The parolee would have the option of doing some sort of education or training, but all their activities would be monitored by Truth Squad officials and the government."

"Okay," I said hesitantly. I waited for the catch. There had to be one.

"Upon completion of their parole, if the parolee has an outstanding parole record, they may choose to either leave or keep working at Truth Squad as a member. By that point, they should have enough training to be a certified member, if they have followed all the rules and applied themselves diligently," Mr. Truth said. "What do you think?"

"I think it sounds like a good program," I replied, trying not to sound too hopeful.

"We haven't officially put the program into motion. We need someone to be our first member of the program. If all goes well, then the program will officially begin, and we will enroll other parolees," Mr. Truth said.

Sarah rolled her eyes. "Basically, he's trying to say that we want you to be our test subject!" she cried excitedly. "Wouldn't that be great?"

"I think so," I replied, unable to keep a smile from spreading across my face. "I would love to do that!"

Mr. Truth smiled. "We already have the government's permission for you to be our first parolee member. There will be a lot of paperwork and agreements that you will have to enter into, but since you're willing, I think that makes it a go."

"Yes!" Sarah said, clasping her hands. "It's perfect."

"When can we start? Maybe sooner than later?" I asked hopefully.

"You can start signing papers today. After Zaiden's trial, you'll come to the Truth Squad campus with us," Mr. Truth replied.

"Sounds good," I said, nodding. *Thank You, Lord, for a second chance*, I prayed silently.

"I'm so excited!" Sarah said, her smile bigger than I'd ever seen. "I can't wait!"

⌐

"We'll be there in ten minutes," Sarah said. She sat in the pilot's seat of her personal aircraft. I sat next to her with Luke behind me.

"I just have one question," I asked, turning to face Luke. "Why didn't Truth Squad help us with the mission? Why were we working on our own?"

"That was two questions," Luke replied, winking.

"Whatever. Can you just answer them?" I asked, smiling.

Luke put a finger to his chin and smiled sneakily. "I don't know ... can I?"

I rolled my eyes.

"Just kidding," he said. "Well, when Truth Squad began, they made an agreement with the government that they wouldn't act without government permission. Both the government and Truth Squad have to be in agreement for us to take on a mission."

"Okay," I replied with a nod.

"So Truth Squad suspected something was up with the PBPC. They asked the government officials if we could investigate, but we were given a no go. We were told that the PBPC wasn't a huge concern at this point; however, they agreed to allow a private organization—one not connected to the government—to investigate further to see whether there was shady business going on," Luke explained.

"So you and Sarah took on the job as private detectives," I said, nodding slowly. "So the FBI wanted you to investigate, but the project wasn't a priority for them."

"Pretty much," Luke replied.

"Why didn't they get involved when you found out about Mr. Zaiden?" I asked.

Luke took a deep breath. "Well, we sent all our information to Truth Squad, who sent it to the FBI. There wasn't enough information in writing for them to get officially involved. We did have enough info through you to take out both the PBPC and Mr. Zaiden, but the FBI wanted us to get more evidence for a solid case."

"It seemed like a solid case to me," I replied.

Luke shrugged. "I thought so too, but rules are rules. Truth

Squad was on standby the whole time, though. The moment we put our final plan in motion, I notified Truth Squad, and they got ready with backup."

"Seriously?" I cried. "And you didn't tell me? I was all stressed out for nothing?"

"Sorry. We didn't really have time. I sent the message as we got out of the car," Luke said.

"Hate to break up this lively discussion," Sarah said, "but we are landing."

"All right! Back home," Luke said excitedly.

I turned back to look out the aircraft's windshield. Below us I saw a landing field with both personal aircraft lanes and jet lanes. Beyond the airplane hangar, I saw a campus with several large buildings, surrounded by acres of wooded property. "Welcome to Truth Squad Airport," Luke said dramatically.

Sarah landed the aircraft and drove it into the hangar. She shut down the plane and then turned to face me. "Ready for your tour?"

🔫

"So, Truth Squad," Luke said, stretching out his hands. "What do you think?"

"I think ... it's awesome!" I exclaimed excitedly. We'd just toured the dorms, the mess hall, the Truth Academy school building, the training rooms, and the woods used for outdoor training. "I can't wait to see how the training equipment works. The technology here is amazing." I smiled.

Mr. Truth walked up to us. "Done with the tour?" I nodded. "Good. Can you come to my office and finish some paperwork?"

"Sure," I replied.

Sarah hugged me before I could walk away. "I'm so glad you're here," she whispered.

"Me too," I agreed, amazed by what God had done to bring my sister and me back together and to bring me back to Him.

Luke shook my hand. "Welcome to the team." He grinned. "Get ready for adventure."

I laughed, feeling right at home. "Good thing I already have experience."

THE END.

Printed in the United States
by Baker & Taylor Publisher Services